Saleena's Dollar

BRANDON YOUNG

BRANDON YOUNG

DEDICATION

In loving memory of Joseph Young JR. You will forever be remembered. I Love You pops!!!

BRANDON YOUNG

BRANDON YOUNG

Acknowledgements

First and foremost I would like to thank GOD.
Without him, none of this would be possible. I
would also like to dedicate this novel to my True
Loving Family and Friends. You all stood by my side
even when I was at my lowest. Thank You!!!!

Saleena's

Dollar

PROLOGUE

Sitting in the driver seat of her 2010 Ranger Rover Sport; Saleena let out a muffled cry, as she wiped her teary eyes. She was parked outside of her ex-boyfriend's condo, contemplating on rather or not she should go through with what she had planned. Visions of a drunken Dollar stumbling up the stairs to the front door of his condo with his arms wrapped around her newest enemy, Saleena quickly thought *fuck it*. She grabbed her best friend Kim's butterfly knife from the glove compartment, then hopped out.

"I can do dis. I can do dis." She continued to tell herself, as she slowly walked up the driveway.

She made it to her destination moments later; Dollars 1976 Chevrolet Caprice Classic which was considered his prize possession. Flipping the knife open, she looked up at Dollars bedroom window, just as the lights were being shut out. With a slight smile, Saleena keyed the words **FUCK YOU** on both sides of the car. She then stood back to admire her work. Impressed, but not satisfied, Saleena slashed all four of the 28" tires sitting under the car. She felt better, her smile was wider, but knew she hadn't done enough yet; she wanted badly to hurt Dollar the way she'd been hurt.

Saleena took another glance up at Dollars bedroom window, and locked eyes with her enemy. With a quick roll of her eyes, Saleena tried the driver side door handle. To her surprise, it was open. She began taking her anger out on the ostrich interior, slicing through the seats, the dashboard, even the convertible top. Happy, Saleena slammed the door, and made a run for her SUV.

Before she could get out of the neighborhood good, her cellphone began to ring. The ringtone Papers by Usher, let it be known who was calling. Snatching her phone out of her Louis V bag, she answered, yelling; "what?!"

Dollar let out a laugh, one that irritated the shit out of her. Then said in his down south slang that truly comes out when he's mad; "I see yuh still on dat lil girl shit. Bitch grow da fuck up! Find yuh uh man and leave me da fuck alone. I'm through wit' chu. Yuh hea' me?! I'm done."

Dollar hung up, but Saleena was determined she would get the last word. She called back, let it ring a few times then the voicemail picked up. Saleena hung up.

"Eww, I hate chu!!!" Saleena yelled out to no one, as she tried calling back.

Frustrated, and trying to figure out what she was going to tell Dollar, Saleena paid no attention to the red light she was quickly approaching. By the time she did, it was too late. Passing through the four ways, a Chevrolet Silverado 3500 rammed the driver side of Saleena's Range Rover. Saleena watched in horror as her Range

Rover spun around twice, then screamed while being pushed into a light pole. Saleena was knocked unconscious due to the impact from the crash....

CHAPTER 1 SALEENA

Shit's been crazy since my pops died ten years ago. My mom went ballistic, started smoking crack, and was found dead not even six months after we buried our pops. True enough I was hurt, but my big brother Dave kept me straight, and keeps me straight. He picks up the slack from both of our parents. Saying I'm spoiled would be an understatement; big bro takes damn good care of me. Keeps me draped in the newest fashions, and I only must ask once to do things.

Only thing he stresses, is how bad he wants me to finish school. Not that he has to, but he makes sure I get to school; literally. Between him, and his girlfriend Rochelle, they take me to school, and when it's over one will pick me up. Big bro claims it's to make sure my ass graduate, and become a doctor, or a lawyer, and not just another dope boy bitch. In my eyes though, that's hardly the case.

At sixteen, I have a mind frame of a twenty-year-old, and a body to match. Standing at 5'4", I'm blessed with a 34c-24 40 frame, caramel complected skin, a chubby face with dimples, a pearly set of white teeth, and some greenish grey eyes. Now you tell me why he keeps a tight leash on me, my point exactly! No matter how many times I try to tell him I'm not fucking, which I'm not. He continues to hound my ass.

The neighborhood where we stay, (**West Savannah**), is considered the slums. Rated high on violence, and drug dealing; something Dave tries to keep me away from. But how the hell can you keep me away from something I was born into. My granddaddy was a d-boy, my pops was a d-boy, and my brother is a d-boy with ten years under his belt. Having the work in the hood, he gets much respect around the way, and that sometimes seems more like a curse, then a blessing; it's like I always got eyes on me and can never do anything without it getting back to Dave.

He never knew it, but he's the one who introduced me to the game. I would never forget that day. It was the first time I saw large amounts of marijuana, and cocaine. My first time seeing, then counting ten thousand dollars. It was also the day my boyfriend and I made it official.

I can remember it like it was earlier this morning. I was nine and was just promoted to the fifth grade. Had all A's and B's on my report card and was ready to show my brother. Dave had his girlfriend Rochelle pick me up from school, because he had business to attend to. The second she dropped me off, I shot up the stairs, and burst through the door with much excitement.

What was sitting on the coffee table wasn't on my mind at first. I just sat down on the couch next to him and handed him my report card. "Bro look!! Straight A's, and B's!!!"

"Dat what's up." While Dave was looking at my report card, he was oblivious to the fact that I was no longer paying him any attention. My focus was on the glass table in front of us. "Keep doin' what you are doin'."

My hands were moving before I could stop them. I grabbed an ounce of cocaine in a sand which bag, and asked with my lil curious ass, "what's dis? It looks like sugar."

"Girl gimme dat!" Dave snatched the bag out of my hand. "Don't ever let me catchu fuckin' round wit' dis shit."

"What 'bout dis?" I was holding up a pound of marijuana, that I later found out was purple haze.

"Dat neither. Put it back." Dave went into his front right pants pocket, pulled out a huge knot of money, then tossed it in my lap. "Go in your room and count dat. You get it right; I'm going to give you half."

Looking at the knot of money, I jumped to my feet; "Aight!!"

Within an hour, I had the total of $10,000.00. It took some time, because I kept miss counting, trying to count it all at once. When I split it up, it became easier to count. I headed back up front to give Dave his money, to find Dave knocked out asleep on the couch. There was a lit blunt sitting in the ashtray on the table in front of him; I grabbed it and hit it a couple times. My coughing brought him out of his high sleep.

"'Leena baby you are trippin'". Dave was patting my back. "You, ok?"

"I just wanted to see what would happen." I continued to cough, as I handed Dave his money. "Dat's ten thousand dollars."

Dave smiled at me; "you right. So, what I owe you?"

"Half of ten is five. You owe me five thousand dollars."

"I got you." Dave pulled off twenty dollars and gave it to me. "I'm giving you dis now, and I'm going to hold da rest for you. How much I owe you?"

I grabbed the pen, and the pad that was sitting on the table. Doing my math, I confidently stated, "four thousand nine hundred, and eighty dollars. Can I go to da stoe?"

By the smile on his face, I could tell he was happy for me. "Yea you can go. But come right back. Do I need to come with you?"

"It's only two buildings ova." I was making my way out the door. "I'm going to be good."

Just like that, I was out the door; skipping every other step until I made it to the bottom. It was hot as hell outside, but the Fell wood Projects was thick as usual. Hustlers were out hustling, the hood basketball players were on the court balling, but I decided to go two buildings over to see Ms. Shirley: the hood candy lady. When I made my way back to my building, Kim, who I consider my best friend was sitting on the last step leading up to my apartment. Sitting down next to her, I handed her my bag of chewies.

We talked for a few minutes and ate candy; that's when I noticed him walking down the sidewalk bouncing his basketball. For a ten-year-old, he was tall, skinny, and black as charcoal. He had the nappy mini afro with the temp fade, and a razor-sharp line up. He stayed fresh; the grey Jordan basketball shorts, and the white tank top went perfectly with the white and grey IX Jordan sneakers he had on. He was a young lookout boy for my brother but told me he was going to make it to the NBA and make me his wife. I was in love with me some Dollar, but y'all know I had to put up one big ass front.

"Girl dey go Dollar." Kim blurted out, as she ate most of my candy.

"And." I mumbled, looking down at my feet.

"Quit frontin', you know you like him."

"Whateva. No, I don't.

"What up 'Leena." Dollar said as he approached us.

The half smile he presented, when I looked up, I couldn't stop myself from blushing. "Hey."

"Well, I'm 'bout to go." Kim jumped to her feet; "y'all be easy."

"Ok girl bye;" I was locked all the way into Dollar, with the cool aid smile plastered on my face.

"A 'Leena;" Dollar was staring me straight in my eyes, standing right in front of me. He had this dead serious mug on his face. While he dribbled his ball from one hand to the other.

"What Dollar?"

Dollar sat down on the step next to me. Pulling this gold ring out of the pocket of his shorts, he asked; "You wonna be my girlfriend?"

Without even thinking, I quickly answered; "yea, I'll be your girlfriend!"

"Good." Dollar grabbed my right hand, put the too big ring on the wrong ring finger, and kissed my lips.

"What da hell y'all down dey doin'?" Dave asked from the top of the stairs.

"Nonthin'." We both said in unison.

The ringing of my cellphone brought me out of my trance, and I had to laugh. The ringtone Love, by Keyshia Cole let it be known who was calling, Dollar. I had to stop doing my hair in the bathroom mirror and run to my bedroom where my cellphone was. Sitting down on the bed, I snatched my phone up to answer it.

"Hello." I said in my sexiest voice.

"What up wit' chu?" Asked Dollar. "Way you at?"

"At home, just Coolin'. I was doin' my hair."

"Oh, you tryin' to look good for me tonight?"

"You can say dat. Why yo coach ova dey Yellin' at chu?"

"I supposed to be practicing".

"Boy bye. Go get ready for yo game. Imma see you dey."

"Aight. I Love You."

"I Love You too."

Hanging the phone up I set there on the bed for a few seconds, just smiling to myself; thinking. Dollar always has that effect on me. Once I gathered my thoughts, I made my way back to the bathroom to do my hair. I already had my hair in a kinky twist style, with the light, and dark brown weave. I decided to do something different, putting two ponytails in the back, one on both sides, and one up top. You would've thought I was one of those dreads from Miami, and I liked the way I looked; it was different.

After my hair was complete, I went to my room to get dressed. I pulled on some tight ass white Apple Bottom short shorts, a white tank top, and a custom-made navy-blue basketball jersey. It had Dollars number 14 on the front, and on the back; it also had his name on the back in white. The navy blue, and white Jordan socks, along with the navy blue and white XIII Jordan sneakers blended well, setting the outfit off. I took one last look in the mirror and decided to show a little stomach; I pulled the jersey up over my pierced navel and tied it at the back. Then I was ready to go.

CHAPTER 2 DOLLAR

Man, I started running through the streets as a young nigga; I was a lookout man at 9. I wasn't just looking out for the police, but where niggas hide their stash, and looking for a nigga to drop something valuable on the ground; shit I was for real about watching my surroundings, had a mind frame of getting rich, even back then. I'm Kevin Dollar, known to Savannah as Dollar Bill. Not only am I known for selling crack in the hood, looking good wherever I go, staying fresh, and getting to that dollar; I'm the Michael Jordan of my era. I'm the truth with that rock.

I'm seventeen, in the eleventh grade, and got more colleges on my dick, then I do females; that's a lot. Most of my homeboys dropped out in middle school, but me shit I couldn't. School is like a fashion show, who could be the sharpest from head to toe, and that was right up my alley. I hustled for my own, so I was always up to date on the fashion trend. Coordinating my gear was nothing, Queen Dollar taught me well.

Her, and my pops Larry Dollar met back when they were in high school. Queen was a cheerleader, who fell in love with a dope boy that ended up being the brains behind the Dollar Cartel. Neither of them finished high school; they both dropped out, and moved to Savannah, Ga. from Miami, Fla. when Queen ended up pregnant with my brother Chuckaboy. After seeing the money that could be made, Pops set up shop, with a nice run ahead of him.

Five years into his run I came along, and 8 years into his run, the

Dollar Cartel was ambushed, then shutdown by the Feds. They gave my pops, along with his three brothers several life sentences for many different charges. My mother, my brother, and I were left on stuck. The Feds took everything, froze all the accounts, and the jack boys took all the money pops was supposed to have put up.

We ended up staying in Fell wood projects; we were shooting that bad. Not wanting to grow old there, my brother jumped off the porch, and started hustling. He was young, but eager; the things I used to do, I learned from him, just perfected that shit. At thirteen, Chuckaboy hit the stash of a peon, and got himself shot in the leg. Chuckaboy caught a murder charge for killing him; that turned into a life sentence with the possibility of parole. I ended up being the lil bad ass nigga running through the projects trying to get into something, and just so happen to be in the right place at the right time.

I was coming out of Ashley's, the corner store on Augusta Avenue, and Hill Street, in West Savannah. This old head who I knew to hustle in the hood, he came running past me. As he did, he dropped an ounce of cocaine in a sand which bag on the ground and kept on pushing. I picked it up, and looked in the direction where he was headed, then where he was coming from. Half a dozen Chatham Narcotic's Team members, better known as CNT, or the jump out boys; they were heading straight toward me.

Thinking quickly, I remembered what my brother once told me. "Hold da dope in your draws, dey won't search you if you don't run." Ducking back into the store, I did just that. After putting it right under my nut sack, I left the store, and headed back to the projects.

Making it back to the projects I noticed Dave sitting in a chair at the top of the stairs of his apartment.

I walked up the stairs and went straight to him. The niggas who were mean mugging me, I mean mugged them back. I felt like I had a reason to be there, and the cocaine I was holding was my way out of the projects. I had hoop dreams of becoming a NBA player, but I knew they were just dreams; I didn't know anybody who made it, but I kept hope alive.

"What up young nigga?" Dave curiously asked.

"You been by da stoe uh minute ago?"

"Yup. Why what up? Dem peoples didn't send you ova here did dey?"

"Neva dat cuz. I know snitches get stitches. I picked dat up for you."

Dave smiled and stood up; "come on."

I followed him inside of his apartment, and after he closed the door, I pulled the coke out, then gave it to him.

"What dey call you young nigga?" Dave tossed the bag on the glass table, then sat down on the leather couch sitting in front of it. "Sit down." He instructed.

"Dey call me Dollar." I sat down next to Dave and started looking around the apartment. It was plush, d-boy style for real; had the best of everything.

"Dollar." Dave repeated, as he pulled out a big knot of money from his pants pocket. Flipping through it, he pulled off a $100.00 bill, and gave it to me. "Come see me tomorrow. I might have uh job for you."

And just like that, I was put in the game as a lookout boy. After I hit several different niggas stash, and call myself trying to hustle, Dave put a fifty slab of crack in my hand. I didn't look back since; I went from a 50 pack to an 8 ball, to a quarter ounce, then a half ounce, a whole ounce, a 4-way, and now I'm buying a 9. I'm getting to that dollar for real; got hustlers in the projects, shopping with me.

"A nigga tighten up."

My one, and my only friend Marcus slapped me in my chest, knocking me out of my meditation mode. Pulling my headphones off my head, I let them dangle around my neck, allowing Young Jeezy to blast out loud. Marcus reached out to grab my hand and pulled me up to my feet.

"Nigga it betta be time to go." I grabbed my gym bag out of my locker, and placed my I-Pod, along with the headphones in it. I then put it back into the locker and locked it.

"Dollar; Pain!" Coach Tucker yelled into the locker room. "Bring y'all asses on!!!"

"You ready to smash dem niggas?" Asked Marcus, as we walked out of the locker room.

"Damn right I'm ready." I dapped Marcus up, then we jogged across the basketball court, and out the door to where the bus was waiting.

The team shot the shit about nothing the whole ride to the Savannah State University, where the rival game between my high school, West Savannah High, and East Savannah High, was to be held. My mind was on winning the game, so I could get to the projects, and make me a few stacks. They didn't seem to get serious about the game, until we burst through the tunnel, and made our way to the court. As usual, the gym was packed, and the crowd was going crazy. I spotted my mom in the stands cheering next to my girl, and after throwing them the deuces, I started warming up, as I looked for scouts.

"Let's bring it in!" Coach Tucker yelled clapping his hands. Once we all got into a circle, he continued; "this is a big one. We need this game. Are you with me???"

"Yeah!!" We yelled in unison.

"Who are we!?"

"Bulldogs!"

"Who are we!?"

"Bulldogs!"

"Hands in. What we going to do on three. One. Two. Three."

"Win!"

I had the crowd jumping and screaming. We were on a 16-0 run, and I scored all 16 points. It was the third quarter, with two minutes left; we were up 65-40. Dribbling the ball down the court, I tried to hear what coach T was yelling, but I couldn't hear anything over the loud crowd. Crossing up my opponent, I shook him up real nice, then I set myself up for a three-point shot at the top of the key. Taking the shot, I scored, and jumped back on defense; I ended up stealing the ball.

"Call time out! Call time out." Coach Tucker yelled.

"Time out." I told the referee and took off to the sideline.

Thirty seconds later, we were back on the court. I decided to slow the ball down, let the time run a little bit; I dished the ball out to the point guard, and he passed it back. Seeing an opening, I took it to the rim, and went up to dunk it; I caught an elbow to the nose.

"Ooooh!" Yelled the crowd.

I pushed the shit out of him, and he had the audacity to swing on me. He caught me good, dead in my mouth. Why did he do that? Hitting him with two jabs to his face, it popped off. At first, it was just the two basketball teams fighting, that is until the projects jumped off the bleachers.

Shit got crazy, quick, and it was no longer a fight between schools. It was between West Savannah, and East Savannah. The police rushed in, and everybody went running their separate ways. They were trying to make it to the exits, but the basketball teams could not leave; we were told to wait in the locker-room, until the police cleared the   parking   lot.

CHAPTER 3 SALEENA

Sitting in the driver seat of Dollar's 2005 Chevrolet Tahoe, I was wondering when Dollar was going to step out the side door of the West Savannah High Schools gym. I had my right-hand girl Queen Dollar with me, cooling in the passenger seat. She was firing up one fat ass blunt of purple haze reefer, so I knew I would be all right in a minute. But I wanted to see my man, and I was ready to get my pussy ate. Before sitting up all night wondering if he is ok, while he is posting up selling crack all-night.

"Here 'Leena;" Queen passed the blunt to me, bringing me back from the crazy thoughts I had running through my mind. As I took a good pull, she said, "that's that good right dey."

With the smoke in my lungs, I inhaled a couple times, and said, "you right, it is." I was trying to hold it, but could not, and I started coughing. Passing the blunt, I got myself together. I was coughing so hard, my eyes were teary, and blurry. As they cleared, I saw Dollar walking, talking with his coach, heading in our direction.

I was in my element. I laid my back into the cushion, got the blunt from Queen, and hit it sexy like, as Dollar got into the backseat.

"What up with y'all." Dollar sat his gym down on the floor and closed the door. He then winked at me, forcing me to smile.

"You, ok?" Queen turned in her seat to look around the seat at Dollar.

I passed Dollar the blunt, and he put on a fake smile as he said, "yea I'm good."

"Den I'm good." Queen turned around in her seat, "'Leena, you can drop me off at da house."

"Aight." I started the ignition and pulled out. "And way you going Mike Tyson?"

"Man take me to da projects." Dollar pulled a thirty-eight snub nose revolver from his waistline and sat it in his lap. "I got to get to dat dollar.

I did not even bother saying anything. I figured by the time I drop Queen off, smoked a couple of blunts, and listened to his wining, I will get what I want. And if that do not work, hell I will suck his dick like he taught me to. I just wanted to spend time with him whenever I could; knowing I had a curfew, and Dave will snap if I am late.

Pulling into the circular driveway of Queens new home, I looked over at Queen, and said, "I am going to call you sometime tomorrow. Kim coming back in town for Spring break, and she say she wanted to do something."

"Oh ok. Just hit my phone, and we will get together." Queen opened the SUV door, and turned her attention to Dollar, who was also stepping out of the SUV. "Call me when you get settled in, I am not in da mood to argue. I know you going to do what you wonna do anyway. Just be safe, ok?"

"Aight." Dollar gave Queen a slight bear hug, and a kiss on her cheek; "I got you."

"Boy get off me." Queen shook Dollar off her; "goodnight y'all."

"Goodnight." We both said in unison.

As I pulled out of the driveway, I had no idea where we were headed. The projects were where Dollar wanted to go, but the furthest thing from my mind. I wanted to feel him licking my pussy. Cranking up the volume to the stereo system, cater to you, by Beyoncé, sung to us. Well, me, because I was willing to do anything for Dollar at that moment. All he had to do is ask. I was feeling that good.

"Man, way we going? I told you take me to da projects. "Dollar noticed I was taking the long way through the city, rather than the southwest bypass, to head to West Savannah.

"And I want to spend some time with chu!" Tossing Dollar a blunt, I continued; "so roll up, and chill out. You going to get there."

No words were needed to be spoken; he knew what time it was. He rolled up a blunt of some purple haze, and as he lit it up, his cellphone began to ring. The ringtone Rubber band man, by TI, let me know it was money calling. By the end of the conversation, I would know how my night would end. Whenever he made money, he would be happy, and throw a few dollars, but whenever he takes a loss he complains about it, and I would have to take him to the projects without catching me a nut.

"What?! Man, I'm on my way." Dollar closed his cellphone and looked at me. "Take me to da projects."

The seriousness in his voice, and the shit I saw in his eyes told me something was not right. So, I asked; "What's going on?"

"Lil Rock got wet up." Dollar had let the blunt go out, so he put fire to it, and hit it hard. "Shit 'bout to get crazy 'round here."

"Boy don't do nothing stupid."

"Man, I am thinking 'bout getting money. Somebody going to handle it."

Whateva nigga, I thought to myself. He said that to fast; just wanted to shut me up. But I rolled with it. When I pulled up in the projects, I rode the streets of the different project houses until I reached Dollar's apartment. Parking in front of it, I threw the SUV in park, and for a few minutes we talked.

After a few quick kisses, Dollar hopped out. Grabbing my cellphone out of my bag, to check the time, I noticed I had a few missed calls. All from Kim.

I called Kim back, and after the third ring she picked up; "bitch way you at? I am at da airport."

"I am on my way now bitch! Bye." I hung up and rushed to the airport to pick my girl up.

CHAPTER 4 DOLLAR

As soon as I stepped out of the truck, and started walking up the stairs, niggas were telling me what happened to Lil Rock. I heard all the stories that was being told, but I was not really paying attention; I continued walking up the stairs to my trap. When I stepped in, I was hit in the face by thick clouds of dark grey smoke. (Kane, Mailman, and Gold mouth); they were three of the niggas in my hustle circle, they were not my friends, but niggas I grew up with. I knew they would cut my throat at any time, but believe me, I stayed strapped up, and on point; they were in there blowing it down.

We were getting money together, slowly taking over the projects together. (Kane), that nigga 21, and been putting in work when I first moved to the projects. (Mailman), he 18, and just got out of YDC, from doing four years; he took a charge for Kane, and when he got out, Kane put him in the game. (Goldmouth), he 19, but was selling crack back when I was just a lookout boy. The only thing we all have in common, is the fact that we cop work from the same person.

Every month, for the past sixth months, we have been going in to purchase a kilo of cocaine from Dave. It comes out cheaper that way; the more weight you buy, the sweeter the price is, and the more money we make. Everybody gets nine ounces and must be ready to re-up when it is that time. I cannot speak for them, but I have been getting to that Dollar. The nine zones I get, I cut it up with baking soda, and cook up at least 12 big ass cookies, then sell them all for a stack: depending on who's the shopper.

"What up with y'all niggas?" There is a leather couch sitting up against the wall to the right, when you enter the apartment; I sat down next to Kane. Mailman, and Gold mouth were already sitting on a couch against the wall across from us.

"I'm cooling' cousin." That came from Gold mouth. He was dumping the guts from a Swisher Sweet cigar, to roll up some reefer he had in a sandwich bag. It was sitting in his lap.

"Just another day in da neighborhood for me." Said Mailman, as he jumped to his feet tucking his 40 caliber on his waistline. Making his way to the door, he continued. "It's time to get back out dey though."

"Dey say dey caught up with him leavin' Savannah State." Kane leaned back into the cushion and looked at me. "Nobody knows who did it, but dem young niggas ain't got no understandin'. Dey out dey tryna wet some shit up. I fuck wit' Lil Rock, he been cool people, but shit I got a family to take care of, and I can't do dat chasin' dat nigga killa."

Gold mouth passed me the blunt, and as I hit it, I said, "I feel dat. I ain't really tryna jump out dey in dat either. It is fucked up doe. Shit been jumpin' today?"

"Yup. Niggas been beaten' da doe down all day." Kane jumped to his feet, tucked his P89 semi-automatic on his waistline, dapped me up, then Gold mouth. He headed to the door; "I'm 'bout to holla at uh few people, den take it in. Y'all niggas hold it down."

It did not take long for Gold mouth to take off, and I laid back on the couch, smoked on a blunt of purple haze as I relaxed a little bit. I was so tired and high, I dozed off. The beating on the burglar bars woke me up, and I sat up to get my thoughts together. The beating continued, so I grabbed my 38-snub nose from under the couch cushion and went to see who was at the door.

"Fuck with me Dollah." Tron said through the burglar bars; "I got eight hundred for you now. I will owe you two. What up?"

"Give me uh minute."

I closed the door, and went past the couch, turned right, and went down the hall where the two bedrooms were. Unlocking the deadbolt lock on my door, I stepped inside. There was another deadbolt lock on my closet door, and after unlocking it, I bent down in front of the floor mounted safe; after punching in the code, I waited the few seconds it took for it to open. In the safe, there were three shelves; I kept some of my money stacked up on the bottom shelf, I used the second shelf to house my reefer, and my crack. The first shelf is where I kept my jewelry. Doing a quick inventory, making sure everything was accounted for, I grabbed a cookie of crack, locked everything up, and went back up front.

"Come on with it." I reached my hand through the bars and got Tron's $800.00. I then gave him the cookie; "I want my two hundred dollars nigga."

"Come on cousin, ya already know I got chu." Tron took off down the stairs.

I sat down on the couch and rolled up another blunt. Visions of the fight in Savannah State gym popped into my mind, then came thoughts of Lil Rock. That young nigga there was hell, trained to go for real; he jumped out the stands, and the projects came right behind him. The projects going to miss him too; and it was all my fault. I popped that off, and here I am kicking back in the trap, saying fuck that, I am trying to get money. A, it is what it is, casualties of war.

Just as I was lighting up my blunt, somebody beat the burglar bars. With my thirty-eight in hand, I opened it, and saw a smoker looking around biting down on her fingernail. She was known around the hood to be very conniving, always wanting to smoke, but never have any money. I hit the blunt hard, and said, "what up?"

"Let me get something." She looked at my face, then down to my dick. "I will take care of you. Take loving care of you."

"If you ain't got no money Maxine, I can't help you."

"I will suck your dick so good. And put dis pussy on you."

"Take dat shit dey down da block, I need money woman."

With that being said, I closed the door, and sat back down on the couch to finish my blunt. She continued to beat on the door, but got the picture, and left after a few minutes. I looked at the time on my Marc Jacobs wristwatch, noticed it was a quarter past eleven, early for a Friday night. Those junkies would be beating the block around 12:30-1:00. That is when most of their money get spent; they get together, put in to buy some crack, smoke it up together too fast, then their back out to cop some more.

The shit I be having alright, despite the fact I whip the hell out of it. The J's love it though, and a lot of them niggas trapping through the projects copping from me. My cookies big, and they know if I step on the porch holding, I am giving out French fries. I fuck with the projects though; if a nigga hungry I do not mind feeding him, and showing love is how I've been surviving so long. I am a young nigga making more money than most of the OG's out here; while them other niggas playing with that dope, fucking up their money, I am stacking mine. Got my own whip, and I am buying my mom's home; at seventeen I'm straight.

In the past eight months, I stacked up damn near $100,000.00, and by the time I graduate, I say I should have about $500,000.00. That is if I could bypass that concrete jungle, and the gangster Paradise. At the rate I am going with this school thing, I should be balling in college. God's will I make it to the pros, and I'll be able to keep my word to 'Leena about making her my wife.

'Leena; just the thought of her put a smile on my face. We been together now for seven years, and I cannot wait to tear that ass up. I will never put any pressure on her, I understand the fact that she is not ready. Besides, I get my rocks off on a regular; a lot of females want to sex me. Standing at 5'9", I am Black as charcoal, 189 solid, shoulder length jet black dreadlocks, and sixteen solid gold teeth.

They consider me a good catch; NBA first round draft pick when I finish college. It has been said I have a few things to learn, that is why I cannot go straight out of high school. So, until then.... I will be trapping.

Bam, bam, bam.... bam, bam.... bam, bam....

And that is exactly what I have been doing, trapping. The last time I looked at my watch, it was 11:15. The sun just came up, and I have not been asleep yet.

"What up my nigga." I opened the door, blocking the sun with my left hand, and my right hand glued to my thirty-eight.

"You still working?" Tron asked handing me $200.00 through the burglar bars.

"Yup. Why what up?"

"I need another one, I got a rack. Dat shit thumping ova dey by Grant Center."

I have been serving Tron for a while, and he has always been a good hustler. Always Loyal and was consistent. "Listen, I ain't got nothing but two left. Dis what imma do for you. I'm going to give you both of them for fifteen."

"Nigga where dey at?!" Tron went into his pocket and pulled out a knot of money. "Dis thirteen. I owe ya two."

I counted out $1,000.00 and gave Tron the rest. "I ain't going to leave you broke my nigga. Just fuck with me when you get it. I will be right back."

Once I grabbed the two cookies I had left, I gave them to Tron, and went back to my room to count my money. Grabbing a book bag from under the king size bed, I stuffed it with the $21,000.00 I counted, then pulled my cellphone out of my pocket, and called 'Leena.

"Hello." I could tell she was not fully awake yet; she still had that frog in her throat.

"Good morning."

"Good morning."

"You going to come get me?"

"Yea. Where you at?"

"Same place you left me. Da trap."

"I'm on my way now."

"Bet dat up. I Love You."

"I Love You too Dollah."

CHAPTER 5 SALEENA

It is my birthday, I can cry when I want to, wine when I want to. And that is exactly what I was doing on my 17th birthday. I was so excited; my brother went out and bought me one of those E350 Mercedes-Benz convertibles. It was a 2007; candy apple red, with tan leather interior, and it was all mine. The first thought came to mind, was the way I am about to stunt on all those little hating ass hoes, who already couldn't stand me.

I love to piss them off, and I don't know why, I just love it how they drool when I walk by. It has been like that for me for years. Big bro has been spoiling me rotten, I do not want for anything. Dave voluntarily put stacks in my pocket around the clock, and tell me to spend that shit, it's no telling when the folks going to come and take it. So that is what I do, that's my job, and I love it.

It is nothing to spending $10,000.00 a week on clothes, and jewelry. My closet stayed filled with Baby Phat, Apple Bottom, True Religion, D&G, and Louie V. Whatever was hot, I was checking it out.

"You like it baby girl?" Dave knocked me out of my trance; he was standing next to me with a big smile on his face, looking at the car in front of us.

"Hell yeah!" I jumped up and wrapped my arms around Dave's neck; "Thank you so much!!!!"

"You are good. But I don't wonna see no niggas driving dis car, I don't want chu riding with too many people. And please stay your ass out of trouble."

I unwrapped my arms from around his neck and stuck my hand out. "I will not. Keys please."

"Ok now." Dave gave me the keys, and I rushed over to hop into the driver seat. Oblivious to the fact my home girl Kim, who I consider my sister, was standing in the doorway drooling like the rest of them hating hoes.

I played around a little bit, learned how to work a few things, and was about to take it for a spin. Realizing I was dressed in the sweatpants, and a tank top I went to sleep in, I hopped out, and rushed inside, through the kitchen, the living room, and down the hall to my room. Kim was laid out across my bed, I thought she was asleep, so I shook her shoulder to wake her.

"Girl get up, and get dressed! We 'bout to hit da streets in my vert!" I was already in my walk-in closet, going through my clothes.

"Way we going?" Kim said with more enthusiasm than she felt; she was slowly getting out of bed.

"I don't know. Way you wonna go?" I tossed my outfit on the bed, took a step back to admire my taste in coordination, and smiled.

"Let us hit da beach. See who out dey." Kim was moving with excitement; the thought of catching herself a d-boy, that would wine and dine her, had her going through the suitcases she had brought with her trying to find her sexiest outfit.

"Cool. I am 'bout to hop in dis water right quick...."

The whole time I washed, I thought about Dollar. That nigga has not called me all morning, and that is not like him. He usually wakes me up, I pick him up from the trap, then drops him off at Queens house. I continued to think to myself, what is with the change of plans? Thinking something might have happened, I made my shower a little quicker than normal.

Wrapped in only a towel, I walked out of the bathroom, and into my room. Kim was laid out on my bed, wrapped in a robe, talking on my cellphone. I did not think anything of it; I started applying lotion to myself. By the time Kim ended her call, I had on some too short, and tight blue jean shorts, by D&G, some white socks with the red rim, and some white and red Airmax 90's.

"Let me see dat phone." I pulled on my red and white pastel bathing suit top and got my phone from Kim. "Bitch chu playing, you betta get dress."

"It ain't going to take me long." Kim jumped up and began to get dressed.

I dialed Dollar's phone number, listened to it rang a few times, then I got the voicemail. I hung up. Within seconds, he called me back; "hello."

"Happy Birthday!" said Dollar.

"Thank you; way you at?"

"Posted up coolin' blowin' on dat gas."

"Oh, ok. Dat explains why I ain't got my early mornin' phone call. You ain't never left da spot."

"Nope. I been getting your birthday money up. You know ya lil ass expensive. What chu got going on today though?"

Damn why this dude always says the right thing? I was blushing, then I smiled from ear to ear. Dollar really had me messed up. Not only did he treat me like I thought I should be treated, but he also thought he had to keep up with Dave, and splurge on me. It was no telling what he had up his sleeve, but I could only see diamonds. I love diamonds; well, I hope he bought diamonds.

"We are going out to da beach, but what chu buying me for my birthday?"

"I ain't buying your spoiled ass shit." Dollar laughed, "I'm through spending my money on you."

"Whateva nigga. I was going to give you some tonight, but o well." It was my turn to laugh.

"A I was just bullshittin." Dollar began copping deuces. "You know I copped chu somethin' real nice. What time ya comin' out?"

"'bout thirty minutes. Why? We meetin' up somewhere?"

"Yea I am going to catch up with you on Victory. I have to pick my car up from Skips. He on Skidaway Drive."

"Dat what's up. You be safe baby."

"I will."

"Bye."

"Bye."

When Dollar, and I hung up, I sat there on the bed for a second picturing me, and Dollar on our wedding day. Him in his all-white tux, with the gold accessories; me, in my tan gown, with the gold accessories. Kim as my maid of honor, Marcus as Dollars best man.

"Snap out of it." Kim was standing in front of the full-length mirror, letting her hair down, as she smiled at me.

"I was just thinkin' 'bout Dollah crazy ass." I was on my feet, pulling a short white t-shirt over my head. Across the front in red, was the words Bad Bitch.

"What you think he got you for your birthday?" Kim was following behind me down the hall, and towards the kitchen, where the door to the garage was.

"It ain't no tellin." As I stepped into the garage, I noticed Big Bro wiping down his 1968 Buick Grand Sport convertible. It was pearl white, with white guts, sitting on big 26" rims. I headed straight to the driver door of my Benz. "Bro you 'bout to hurt a lot uh dese niggas feelin's dis summer wit' dat one. It looks good."

"Appreciate it. Y'all be good. Call me if ya need me."

"We will." We said in unison.

As I started the ignition, I threw Dave the deuces, then pulled out of the garage. Before I could back out into the street, we were blocked in, by a dozen or more police cars. I was told by one of the officers to kill the engine and step out of the car; that is exactly what I did. Every other officer, other than the one keeping Kim and I posted up by a squad car, they rushed into the house. Every one of them were sporting FBI.

Not even ten minutes past, and the Feds were bringing Big Bro out in cuffs. They led him to a police car, and our eyes were locked in the whole time. He mouthed the words; get at Rochelle, she got chu. I just nodded my head, as I tried to keep the tears from coming. Even though I had no idea what was going on, I knew I had to let Rochelle know something.

They stuffed Dave into the car, and I turned my attention to the officer standing in between Kim, and I. I asked, "what's goin' on?"

She told me something about a conspiracy case, my brother being a king pin, and if I knew anything I could go to prison for covering for my brother. I looked at that bitch like she was crazy; there is no way I would tell on my brother. No matter what the situation may be. If it was not for the officer approaching us, I would've snapped on her. He told her something about not finding anything, and most of them piled up and left; a few sat in their cars outside.

As I walked back inside, I could tell it was a wreck. Drawers were left open, and the contents from them were scattered over the floor. We continued to walk through the house, and I pulled my cellphone out to call Rochelle. I was pissed, for so many reasons; we had not been out of the projects a year, and the Feds were already taking the closest person to me, away from me. I shook my head as I dialed Rochelle's number.

"Hello." Rochelle answered.

"Da police just rushed da house. Dey got bro." I was looking at the mess they made in my room.

"'Leena baby listen to me. Get out of there. They are comin' back, and they are going to confiscate everything. Do not worry about bringing nothing with you. I got you. I am on the south, so call me when you get out here."

Rochelle hung up, and for a second, I took in everything I was leaving behind. I wanted to pack up all my stuff, but I knew if Rochelle were right, they would be back, and they would take my car. I was not trying to let that happen. We rushed out of there just like Rochelle said, and after jumping in my whip, we were off in the wind. Making it to the South side, I tried calling Rochelle, but got the voicemail each time. I decided to just head out to Queens house, where I knew I would be welcomed.

CHAPTER 6 DOLLAR

Man, I love this time of the year, Summer. It is hot, but by Savannah being so close to the water, we always have a slight breeze. The ladies come out in damn near nothing, and the d-boys bring their whips out. The hustlers in my generation, down south my way, have an old-school car fetish. I saw a young hustler smashing down Abercorn St., towards the south side of Savannah a few weeks ago; he was pushing a '72 Buick Centurion convertible, mounted up on some 26" rims, sitting up like a monster.

I have been seeing them on the regular, and after seeing over three dozen in a week, I decided I wanted to jump into the old-school game. I was on my hustle double time, wanted to flip me a whip. When it was time to re-up, I pulled up on Dave with $35,000.00, and copped two bricks. I broke those niggas off their nine, dropped my nine with my thirty-six, and added eighteen ounces of baking soda. The dope was 92% pure, so I used that to my benefit. Thirty-three of the sixty-three zones was cooked up, but thirty were sold in powder form.

I tore the projects up with that dope and have been ready to re-up since the middle of last month. So, I have just been cooling laying low, letting my partners catch up. The moment I was waiting for, finally arrived; Orange crush week was coming up, and I was almost ready. People from many states made their way to Savannah, so they could participate in the d-boy get together on Tybee Island. There are always live performances on the beach, by the hottest artist, and a free cookout on the pier. It was like a car show, fashion show, and a swimsuit competition all in one.

I was up early that morning, getting myself together; that thug motivation 1o1 was blasting through the stereo. Don't get caught was playing, and as I looked at myself in the bathroom mirror, I brushed my teeth, while trying to rap along. "Should I stay, should I run. Got hard, got soft, got pills, got guns." I damn near choked on the toothpaste, and stopped rapping, to spit it out in the sink. After rinsing my mouth out with Listerine, I washed my face, then brushed my gold teeth. Getting dressed came next.

Sliding into a pair of white linen shorts, I put on a short sleeve linen button up to match. The all white SAV fitted cap I put on my head was nice and help the low top air forces complement the outfit. Taking a seat on the bed, I started rolling up a blunt of purple haze. In the process of rolling a blunt, my cellphone began to ring. I kept rolling, and by the time I finished, it quit ringing.

Being sure to call 'Leena back, we talked for a few minutes. After hanging up with her, I kicked back, and got high as I waited for Marcus to pull up on me. About twenty minutes later, I heard the slap from an old school trunk, coming up the block. Standing up, I tucked my 40 caliber on my waistline, slid my Gucci gold rimmed frames on my face, then checked myself out in the full-length mirror.

After locking up, I headed outside, and down the stairs to the 1975 Buick LeSabre convertible, Marcus pulled up in. It was navy blue, with white guts, and a white top to match; Nico had it sitting on some 26" rims. Marcus big brother Niko was a well-known d-boy on his side of town, and let Marcus hold his car so he could stunt at the beach.

"Dollah B! What up wit' you round." Marcus dapped me up, as I slid into the passenger seat.

"Shit I'm coolin' brotha." Pulling a blunt out of the box of blunts I saw sitting on the seat when I sat down, I busted it, and threw the guts out the door. Shutting the door, I rolled up some purple haze while Marcus pulled out.

We rode through the streets of Savannah, getting high, and stopped at several jewelry stores so I could cop 'Leena something nice. Then we made our way to Skips, a well-known paint and body shop, on the east side of Savannah. After backing into a parking spot, in front of the office, we hopped out, and headed inside. Skip gave us a warming smile as we entered, and after a few minutes of talking about nothing, we were led through a side door of the office. Stepping into the shop, Skip led us to the back, where my car was.

"Ok. Ok." Walking up to my car, the smile was hard to hold in. The cocaine white paint was candy, and had the light pink pearl in it, resembling the fish scales from the good cocaine we were selling. Opening the driver door to see the interior, my smile widened; Skip had it exactly how I wanted it. The interior matched the top, the paint, and the twenty-six" Asanti rims. "Dat what I am talkin' 'bout. Skip you put uh nigga in da game!!"

"I tol' you I had you." Skip dapped me up.

"Yea she looks good. Real good." Hopping into the driver seat, I started the ignition, and hopped back out. "What I owe you?"

"You already gave me eight. Just give me seven."

Reaching into my pants pocket, I pulled out my money, and was about to pay him. But then I thought about something. My music was not playing, so I asked, "what up wit' my music?"

"I had a switch put in it." Skip walked over to the car, got into the driver seat, and after flipping the switch under the steering column the music came on. "I did it in case you get pulled ova for ya music. Just flip a switch."

"Bet."

I paid Skip his $7,000.00, then hopped into my new toy; a 1972 Chevrolet Chevelle convertible. Then I was off in the streets, with Marcus behind me. We stopped to the gas station, to get some gas, some blunts, and we headed out to the island. I was so excited about showing off my Tonka toy, I forgot I was supposed to catch 'Leena in traffic. To be honest, she was not even on my mind at the time.

For the past couple of years, I have been riding with homeboys, or getting a rental to enjoy orange crush. This was the first year I was riding my own whip and was feeling really good about it. Riding down the strip of Tybee Island Beach, I noticed that year was the deepest of the ones I have been to. The movement of the cars were slow, due to backed up traffic. In every direction I looked, there was someone pulling to the side of the road, trying to stunt in some way.

Hanging out of the sunroof, or the windows. Ghost riding their whip or hopping out to stop up traffic as they listen to their music. The thing that really put the traffic on slow motion, was the fine ass women prancing around in bathing suits, with sandals or heels. There were females everywhere; it was dog heaven. As we cruised through the traffic, I chunked up the deuces at those I knew, and kept on pushing.

Being ready to park, and post up a little bit, I headed over to the beaches parking lot. I wanted to bag a few of those ladies who were waving at me, as I rode down the strip. The parking lot was congested, just like the strip; everyone was riding through, showing their cars off. Finding a parking spot, I waited for Marcus to park next to me, then together we hopped out. Leaving our trunks beating, sounding like two offbeat marching bands, we leaned up against the hood of my car.

Tossing Marcus a blunt, I took off my linen top, and sat it in the backseat. Turning around to take my place in front of the hood, I noticed two sexy ladies strutting by. "What up wit' you miss lady." I directed that to the 5'9", 36c-28 40, redbone. She was sporting this red two-piece bathing suit with the heels to match; "how are you doin' today?"

"I'm alright." She was standing directly in front of me, bowlegged to death. "You?"

"I'm just coolin." Marcus had her girl locked in, so I took flight. I reached out to shake her hand; "dey call me Dollah."

"Nakita."

We were in a damn enjoyable conversation. I was just getting her number, when a candy painted old school truck, sitting up on 26" rims pulled up in front of us. It was Marcus' brother Nico. Marcus headed over there to see Nico, and I threw Nico the deuces. The few minutes Marcus talked to Nico, I continued to chop it up with Nakita, then I let her go her way.

"Bruh!" Markus walked up and passed me a blunt. He was shaking his head, and before I could ask, he said; "dem Feds in town. Dey just knocked Dave out da box."

"What?!?!" Pulling my phone out of my shorts pocket, I noticed I had eight missed calls, and five unread text messages. I wondered why my phone did not ring, and realized it was on silent mode. Without reading the messages, I called 'Leena back.

"Nigga way you at?" 'Leena snapped. "I been calling yo' black ass for hours!"

"My shit been on silent. But fuck all dat, way ya at? You good? I heard 'bout OG."

"Yeah I'm good." She tried her best to put up a front, but I could hear it in her voice, she was only playing tough.

"Aight. Way you at?"

"Yo' house."

"Stay dey. I'm on my way."

It seemed like the crowd was getting thicker by the minute, but it was the least of my worries. Making sure 'Leena was ok was a priority for me. Dapping Marcus up, I hopped in the whip, and mashed out. The speed limit did not slow me down, nor did the cops stop me; I made it home in no time. Pulling into the driveway of Queens home, I peeped a red Benz with a bow on the front, and figured it was 'Leena's birthday gift from OG.

"Ma! 'Leena!" I was calling their names the moment I was in the foyer.

"We are up here!" Queen yelled from upstairs.

Making it up the stairs, I checked the two rooms on both sides of the hallway. Came up with nothing, so I headed to the end of the hall, where Queens room was. 'Leena, Kim, and Queen were laid out in bed watching a movie on the 68" plasma TV mounted on the wall. Seeing me walk in, 'Leena jumped up to greet me.

Wrapping my arms around 'Leena, I squeezed tight as I asked; "you alright?"

"Man fuck no. Dem people talkin' 'bout conspiracy, bro a king pin. And how I can go to prison if I know somethin' and I don't tell. And I thought I had somewhere to go, but Rochelle"

"Hol' up baby." I had to stop her because she was beginning to stress things I already knew. On the ride over, I made a call to Queen, and she told me everything. "Dis ain't da time to get emotional, and crash. True enough, bro gone, but I got your back one hundred percent; whenever you need me." I was staring into her eyes, letting it be known my words were coming from my heart. "Now put ya big girl thongs on. It is crunch time baby."

CHAPTER 7 SALEENA

"Aight." Was all I could say.

That half smile of his, always brings comfort to any situation. But I could not stop myself from wondering where things were going to go from there. In my heart, I knew Dollar would take care of me, well I was hoping he would. I knew nothing about taking care of myself. All my life I have been pampered, and knew things were about to change, but had no idea how much.

Standing on my tippy toes, I slipped him the tongue. Pulling myself away, I attempted to step over to where Queen, and Kim were pretending to watch tv; the light tug around my waist, pulled me back into Dollars arms. Before I could ask a question, he gave me that half smile of his, and I melted. Even started leaking.

"You tryna get out da house?" Dollar asked knocking me out of my thoughts.

"Way, we goin'?"

"Do not matter. You tryna get out the house or not?"

"Hell yea!" Interjected Kim, who jumped out of the bed.

"Cool. Let's ride."

I had no idea where we were headed, and I did not even care too much. I knew I was going to be with my man, and that made me feel good. Following Dollar out the door, I could not stop thinking about Big Bro; true enough he mentioned it, but I never really thought about the FEDS taking him away from me. Now I was forced to grow up and become a woman.

"A you need to put dis in da garage." Dollar was at the passenger door of my car, looking through the window at the interior.

Is dis nigga serious? I thought to myself. I had no intentions on parking my baby in a garage, where she could not be seen. I had just gotten my Benz that morning, had not even had a chance to show her off yet. But I knew there had to be a good reason for Dollar to say some crazy shit like that.

Not knowing, and wanting to know why, I put my hand on my hip, then asked; "why I have to put my car in da garage? I want to drive it."

As I switched my weight from one leg to the other, he leaned against the passenger door of my Benz, and said, "dem peoples going be looking for dis car, and if dey get it, dey ain't giving it back. I know a nigga who will change da numbers, and I will get it painted for you, even sit some shoes up under it, but right now you need to put it up."

There was nothing else needed to be said, I didn't want to lose my car. Not having another idea as to what else could be done with it, I tossed Dollar the keys; "you can do it."

"Here." Dollar tossed me a set of keys, as he got into the driver seat of the Benz. "Start dat up."

Other than my car, there was one more in the driveway. Hopping into the driver seat of the old school, I started the ignition. I had no idea what kind of car it was, but knew it was pretty, sitting on some big rims. I fell in love with the color on sight of it; candy white, with some type of pearl pink in it. It had plush leather guts, and from the growling sound coming from the front of the car, I knew it had to be something serious under the hood.

"Dis shit nice." Kim climbed into the backseat and was looking around at the interior. There were TVs in the headrest, along with the two in the sun visors, one in the review mirror, and a 17" sitting between the two bucket seats that caught her attention. She pictured herself on the passenger side, cruising down I-95 for a second. Wanting to know who it belonged to, she asked; "is it his?"

"I don't know." I was doing my inspection; checking under the driver seat, I found a pistol, and an ounce of reefer. Quickly placing it where I found it, I checked under the passenger, but there was not anything under there. There were a couple of blunts in the glove compartment. As I was taking one out if the box, to bust, Dollar was coming from around the corner of the house; that is where the garages were.

"You good?" Dollar said as I was about to slide in the passenger seat. "You drive."

Without a word, I gave Dollar the blunt, as he got into the passenger seat; then I positioned myself for takeoff. I was about to pull out, when Dollar reached down, pulled the gun, and the reefer, from under the seat. I let him roll up, then I pulled out of the circular driveway, and hit the streets. I never knew driving an old school on big rims drove like a truck; well to me it did. It was sitting up over every other car and made me feel superior; I was pushing their asses out of the way.

On the way to our destination, we made a quick stop to Cloverdale, to meet up with Marcus at his parents' house. Marcus, and Kim bonded instantly; they have seen each other on numerous occasions, Marcus even tried to get with Kim, and was declined each time. I believe it was the old school he was driving, that made this occasion different. She was a little more outgoing, giving flirtatious looks, and did not hesitate to hop into his whip. Bumper to bumper, we headed out to Tybee Island.

Dollar would not let the top back, nor tell me how to do it. He continued to fire up blunt after blunt, and said it was the safest way to ride. I chalked it up, and ran with it, knowing I was fighting a losing battle. The snowballs blowing through the ac unit felt good, but I wanted to feel the cool breeze from the wind. It took us about an hour, to make it to the strip, and I was determined to let everybody see me whipping my man's Tonka toy.

Before I could turn the music down, and ask Dollar to let the top back, he reached over me, and for a second, I thought he was going to grab my thigh. Pushing a button on the dash, the top slid back, and the sun started shining in. Cruising the strip, we caught a lot of attention; the well-known deceased rapper Camouflage has this song featuring Birdman, called Laying My Stunt down. No ideas of what was in the trunk, but we were laying our stunt down on those haters as we rode through letting our trunk slap that 'Flage. Everyone we passed by, were turning their heads our way.

We made our way to the beaches parking lot, and Dollar told me to find a parking spot, so we could post up. Spotting a few empty spaces, next to a few members of Dollars basketball team, I backed in. While Dollar, Marcus, and the other niggas, smoked their reefer, laughed, and gawked at the girls passing by, Kim and I sat on the hood of Dollars car. True enough, I love my girl to death, but I did not want to hear nothing she had to say about Marcus, which was a lot. I was actually mad as hell, and it had nothing to do with her; here it is my B-day, my brother had been locked up, and I actually thought I would be spending time with my man. But that was not happening, and I hadn't even received my gift from that nigga.

Tired of holding my breath, I told Kim, "Hold up real quick." Looking over to where Dollar was, I continued; "Dollah come 'ere."

He looked in my direction and made his way over to the car; standing between my legs, he wrapped his arms around my waist; "what up."

"I ain't feelin' dis shit." Wrapping my arms around his neck, I gave him a quick kiss; "I'm ready to leave babe."

"Aight let me holla at bros real quick." With a quick kiss to the lips, he was gone.

"I'm fuckin' dat nigga tonight."

"What?? Bitch, who?" I was looking her dead in the eyes, hoping she was not about to say what I was thinking. I did not want to fall out with my girl about no dick, but shit Dollar belonged to me. And sharing was not my thing. If only I knew the truth back, then.

"Marcus bitch. Who else?"

Pop pop.... Pop pop pop....

CHAPTER 8 DOLLAR

"What up now nigga?"

The few seconds it took for me to walk over to where Marcus was, I was confronted by a couple of the East Savannah High basketball team players. The one I was fighting with, and one more. Not being fond of talking, I took off on the one who hit me with his elbow in that game; caught him in the mouth and opened him up quick. The same way I caught him, his partner caught me, and Marcus caught him the same way. He dropped to the ground.

Marcus, and I continued to work the first guy; we had him laid out on the ground, but we continued to beat him. Out of my peripheral vision, I noticed his partner pulling something from his waistline, as he came up from the ground; I pulled my forty caliber from my waistline. He let off two rounds and caught Marcus in the shoulder with one; firing off three rounds, I hit him in the chest with one, and as he tried to dive, the other two caught him in his stomach.

The parking lot went crazy; everyone took off running, scattering everywhere. Being concerned about my ace, I went nowhere. Rushing to his side, I stayed there, gun in hand hoping I did not have to bust no one else.

"Baby come on!" I heard 'Leena yell.

My baby had pulled the car next to us, and Kim threw the passenger door open. Helping Marcus into the passenger seat, then the backseat, I kept my eyes open. I knew the police were going to be bum rushing the parking lot soon; the sirens were getting closer, and closer.

"Let's go!" I yelled, and 'Leena pulled out.

As we were pulling away from the scene, I looked down at the ground. The nigga I shot was lying there coughing up blood; all I could do is shake my head. I hated the way that went down.

"You got dat nigga Bro?" Asked Marcus, as he held on to his gunshot wound?

"You damn right I got him." Handing Marcus my linen shirt, I continued; "put pressure on dat shit dey my nigga. We going to get you to da hospital. Baby go to Urgent Care."

"Way da hell dat at?" Asked 'Leena.

"Just drive, I got you."

Sitting back in one of the chairs, in the hospital waiting area, I ran my hands through my shoulder length dreadlocks. I could not stop replaying the incident in my mind. Marcus was rushed into surgery, and we were told he would be ok. That made me feel better, but every time I looked over at his mom's, and pop's, I felt bad all over again; felt it was my fault he was lying in a hospital bed having surgery. His mom's continued to cry and his pop's continued to try and comfort her, but she never seemed to calm down. Nico came in on some murder shit for real and had no understanding about nothing; I didn't bother to broadcast the fact I had put bullets into the nigga who shot Marcus. I figured he would find out one way or another.

"Baby, are you ok?" 'Leena rubbed the back of my neck, to try and relieve the tension.

I turned to give her a fake smile; "It is what it is. I would be betta if dis shit never happened."

"I know babe. Don't beat yourself up about it. When are you tryin' to go home? You look like you need some rest."

"After I make sure my brotha good, we can leave."

We sat there for what seemed to be hours before the doctor came out to speak with Marcus' parents. They were led back to where he was, and after a few minutes, they came out, and I went in. He smiled the minute he saw me; that brightened me up.

"What up wit' you round?" I walked in, and dapped Marcus up.

"I'm just coolin' bro."

"Dat what's up. But you need to hurry up, and get up out dis bitch; you got some seats to clean."

Marcus let out a laugh; I did too. "Nigga damn dem seats, my life was at risk."

"Just uh lil hit to the shoulder. Nothing to serious. What dey talkin' 'bout; when dey letting you go?"

"Couple days. Week at da latest. But dealin' wit' dem people"

The knock at the door, cut him off in mid-sentence. We both turned in the direction of the door, as it opened. It was the last thing I needed at the time, to see the police.

"Marcus Pain." One of the two Detectives said walking in, then he offered, "I am Detective Smith, and this is Detective Jones. We'll like to ask you a few questions. That is if you do not mind."

That was my cue. I said my goodbyes to Marcus, and before the police had a chance to see the blood on my clothes, I dashed out of there. On my way out the door, I looked over to where 'Leena was seated. We locked eyes for a minute, and there was not a thing needed to be said. She got up, and with Kim on her heels, they headed for the door as well. By the time they made it to the car, I was busting a blunt to role.

"You going to tell me what's goin' on?" 'Leena started the ignition, and started to pull out; "or you going to leave me in da blind?"

"Man, dem people up dey talkin' to Bro." I hit the blunt hard, then passed it to 'Leena. "And I don't need no parts of dat."

The ride to Queens house was in silence, other than the music playing through the speakers. I was in my own zone; trying to figure out what was next to come my way. I knew that beef shit wasn't over; I left one alive and knew he would be back to retaliate. Meaning I knew I had to be ready. 'Leena pulled into the circular driveway, and to the back of the house, where the garage was. Pulling into one of the free spots, we hopped out.

The first thing I did when I made it inside, was check on moms. After giving her goodnight kisses, I decided to take me a shower. It was not a real long one, but it was relaxing, and it eased my mind a little bit. I dried off, slid on a pair of boxers, and headed down the hall to my room. Sitting down on the bed, I rolled me another blunt of purple haze.

As I was putting fire to the blunt, there was a soft knock at the door; I said, "come in."

"Damn nigga you kickin' dat anti-social shit now?" 'Leena took a seat on the bed next to me.

"Gon' wit' da games, it ain't nothing like dat." I passed 'Leena the blunt; "Your present up dey on da dresser though."

"We'll get to dat later." 'Leena stood up, locked the door, and put the blunt out in the ashtray, sitting on the nightstand. "Right now...."

She gave me a seductive smile, as she straddled me. She wrapped her arms around my neck, and slowly began to place kisses all over my face. When she pushed me in my chest, it caught me off guard, and I fell backwards into the bed.

"Don't start some shit you ain't gon' finish."

She was licking my earlobe, making her way to my neck; "trust me, I can finish it."

Slowly, she made her way to the other side of my neck, and to my ear. She then kissed my lips, and my chest. Spelling her name on my chest, she had my dick throbbing underneath her. She was kissing and licking her way down the middle of my chest, to my naval.

"Damn, you don' did dis before?" I asked with a smile.

"Shut up boy." She grabbed both sides of my boxers and pulled them down. "Somebody happy to see me huh."

I just smiled as 'Leena licked the head of my dick; that felt so good, and when she covered it with her mouth, shit got serious. 'Leena was wrapping her tongue around my dick as she sucked it. She massaged my balls with one hand, while she braced herself up on the bed with the other. My dick began to throb in her mouth, and I knew it would not be long before I bust one, and I wanted to wait. So, I gently grabbed 'Leena's shoulder, and lifted her up.

"Oh, now you don't want me to finish."

"Come 'ere."

Flipping 'Leena on her back, I lifted her shirt over her head, and began my own lil foreplay. A few kisses on her throat, the nape of her neck, and she was moaning. Seeing that I was on point, I made my way down her breast; one by one I kissed them, then licked around her nipples. That intensified her moans, had her squirming from my every touch, so I moved in for the kill.

'Leena lifted her hips, so I could pull off her panties, and I went to work on that pussy. I sucked, and I nibbled on her clit, while I finger fucked her with my index finger. My middle finger wouldn't fit, her pussy was too tight. I continued to lick her wet, and suck her dry, then she came. Squeezing my head between her thighs, she locked her hands behind my head, and pushed my face deeper into her pussy. Within seconds, she climaxed again.

"Baby I wonna feel you inside uh me." 'Leena wined.

"You sure?" 'Leena nodded her head. "I got chu. It's gon' hurt baby, just be easy. Whateva, you do, don't squeeze your muscles."

"Ok."

Running my dick up, and down the slit of 'Leena's pussy, I lubricated it, then placed it at the entrance of her pussy lips. Wanting to take my time, I eased the head in; she gasped. I pulled out, and slowly pushed it back in, adding a few more inches this time. 'Leena's mouth went wide, like she wanted to scream, but no words came out. Her eyes began to tear up, and her pussy muscles gripped my dick. I stopped penetrating; hell, I stop moving all together, and stared down into 'Leena's eyes.

After a few seconds, her muscles let me go, and I continued to slide deeper, and deeper into 'Leena's pussy. She slowly began to get into it; 'Leena wrapped her arms around my neck, and slowly began to gyrate her hips. She was trying to match my strokes. As I hit rock bottom, that pussy got wetter; I slow stroked, long dicked 'Leena good, then she began to climax. My strokes began to speed up as I felt my nut reaching the top. Just as I was about to pull out, 'Leena wrapped her legs around me.

"I love you," 'Leena was climaxing again.

"I love you too." I was ejaculating inside of 'Leena.

Out of breath, and flabbergasted, we fell onto the bed in each other's arms. 'Leena smiled at me, I smiled at her, then looked down between us; my dick was covered in blood, semi hard, and still leaking. I needed to wash, but I wanted to finish my blunt first. I grabbed the blunt out of the ashtray, lighter off the nightstand, and lit it up.

"You, ok?" I fell back on the bed and looked over at 'Leena.

"I'm good." 'Leena sat up and began getting dressed. "I'm 'bout to wash."

"You wonna hit dis?"

"Nah I'm good, go ahead." 'Leena gave me a quick kiss and headed toward the door. "Holla at me when ya get out da shower."

"Ok."

Putting the blunt out in the ashtray, I got up, and after pulling my boxers on, I headed to the bathroom down the hall. Hearing the water running I figured I would use the one downstairs, and as I turned around, I caught Kim coming up the stairs; she was staring at me. She was looking good in those boy shorts, and that wife beater; I ain't going to lie, my dick started jumping, but I threw the thought out of my mind, and kept pushing past her.

She looked me up, and down, started to say something, but decided against it; I headed down the spiral stairs. When I reached the bottom, I made a left in the foyer, then another left down the hallway, where the guest bathroom was located. After turning on the water in the shower, I relieved myself in the toilet, then hopped in the shower. Stepping out of the shower, I was drying my hair with a towel; wrapping it around my neck, I begin to put my boxers on. Kim's voice caught my attention.

"Ain't no need in doin' dat." She was leaning up against the door naked.

"Oh really?"

"Yep."

Kim was making her way over to where I was. Quickly dropping to her knees, she took my dick into her mouth. My dick responded the way she expected, and the head game was exactly how I heard it was; great. Yes, I knew I was dead wrong, and I should've stopped her. Truth of the matter, I did not want to; she knew what she was doing.

CHAPTER 9 SALEENA

"Push!"

"I am pushin' dammit!"

Nine months of running around with this little guy inside of me, I was ready to get his little ass out. The pain was excruciating; my pussy was actually opening up. My walls were tearing, and this little joker was bucking. Had me regretting the first time Dollar and I had sex, which was the time I got pregnant. Speaking of Dollar, where was he? I went through damn near the whole labor by myself, then he walks his ass in, like everything was all G. "Baby you, ok? You need anything?" I did not say a damn thing, I grabbed his hand, and squeezed.

He was trying to take the pain, be cool about the situation, but I knew my shitty ass attitude was really getting to him. If that did not do it, I knew the tight grip to his hand would. He helped me through my breathing exercises, even wiped my forehead with a cold rag. He was actually getting a few points with me; that is until he told me he loved me.

I was too my last few pushes. As my baby's feet came out, I yelled, "I hate you!" Feeling like I have been tough enough, I slowed my breathing down, and began to cry.

The doctor slapped my baby on the ass, then Dollar cut the umbilical cord. The nurses swaddled him up and was about to leave; Dollar rushed over to block the door, when my baby screamed.

"Hol' up, way ya goin' wit' my baby?" Dollar took Jr. from the nurse, and when Dollar looked down at him, he became quiet.

"We have to clean him, run a few tests. I will bring him back; I promise." Said the nurse.

Dollar looked over at me, caught a glimpse of the afterbirth, and the amniotic sac the doctor was pulling out of me. Handing our pride, and our joy over to the nurse, Dollar began hurling over the floor. Wiping his face with his hand, he made his way back to the bed side. I was damn near asleep.

"You need to clean dat up, don't you think?" I mumbled giving him a weak smile.

"Nah, dey got people who will." Dollar kissed me on the tip of my nose; "get some sleep ma, and I'm goin' to see Jr. I will be back."

"Aight." Was all I could manage to utter.

Just like that, he was out the door; I laid there for a few minutes thinking, mostly about my future. I was expected to graduate in a couple of months, but I had no idea what I wanted to do once that happened. The only thing I was good at, was spending money, and staying fly. I have not looked into any colleges; to be honest, that was the last thing on my mind. I was more concerned about how I was going to take care of little Kevin Dollar Jr.

I knew Dollar had a little money, and was stacking it up heavy, even knew where he kept it, in case something was to happen to him. But I needed my own shit, my own hustle. The question was what type of hustle. I needed some advice, needed it quick, and decided to get it from the #1 hustler I knew: my Big Brother Dave.

The 48 hours I was in the hospital, I plotted up a few things; the conversation I had with Bro was just what I needed, and the advice was on point. Thank God he had him a cellphone in prison; being out in Kansas, I had no idea where he was, and he did less writing as possible. After explaining to him how I had no intentions on punching into anyone's clock, he gave me knowledge about making money. 'Finding something you good at is the biggest thing, Dave stressed, 'I like sellin' work, and I'm good at it. What can you do?'

I thought about it for a minute, then told him about my talent in coordinating clothes, doing nails, and hair. 'Dey, you go, make it happen, and if you need me, get at me.' At that very moment, he hung up on me, and I began to plot. Queen had a Beauty Salon, in the downtown area of Savannah; it was called Queen$ Creations. I figured I could holla at her, on the nails tip, even see if there was a way for me to sell clothes there. Needing clothes to sell, and knowing Dollar stayed sharp, I decided to chop it up with him, and see if he knew where I could get a quantity of excellent quality clothes.

Having everything mapped out, I knew it was time to put my plan into action. On the ride to Queens house, from the hospital, Dollar seemed a bit too quiet. Distant, and as I thought about it, he's been that way for a few months.

"Baby I been thinkin';" I broke the silence, as I looked over at Dollar from the passenger seat of his Tahoe.

"I'm listenin". That nigga did not even take his eyes off the road, to look at me.

"I wonna hustle." That got his attention. He looked over at me, with a raised eyebrow, then turned his attention back to the road.

"And make my own money."

"What you got brewin' up top woman?"

"Well, I know Queen got dat shop, and I figured I could talk to her 'bout sellin' clothes in dey. In da process, I could maybe do nails, to pull my own weight around here."

Dollar leaned back into his seat, sighed heavily, but did not say a word. So, I asked, "what? You 'on't like my idea?"

"Nah, dat ain't it."

"Den what is it? Nigga talk to me!"

"Baby I'm movin' to New York in July."

Talk about raining on my parade, that hit hard, caught me off guard. There I was, 17, just had a baby, and my nigga was about to take flight on us. "What?!" I yelled. I did not mean to, but I woke Jr up. I turned around the seat, to see about him, and after rubbing his stomach, giving him a smile, he calmed down, and slowly went back to sleep.

"I'm goin' to school up dey. I must get my game together. Dats da only way I can go pro. It's like a training camp. Some private owned shit. Dey know 'bout chu, and Jr. I want y'all to come. I have a house already laid out, and everything.

Ok, he may have somethin' here, I thought. A new scenery sounded good, and the house already laid sounded great. But I did not see where my plans fit in. So, I asked; "I see exactly what you saying right, but way my plans come in at?"

"I am already on top of dat. I enrolled you in AIU, and you majoring in fashion design. I want you to open up a clothing line; I'm putting up all da money. If you want me to, I will open you uh nail shop."

He had me then; "fashion," that is my thing, and it caught my attention; the second the words rolled off his tongue. *I could do a fashion show, that's nothing.* I thought. *Just have to create some fly, and different gear, while in school.*

"Ok I'm game. On one condition doe."

"Come on wit' it."

"Instead of uh nail shop, let's do uh clothin' store."

"Done."

"And."

"I thought you said it was only one condition;" Dollar let out a little laugh.

"I am for real, you laughing. You have to take care of Jr. while I am in class."

"Man, dat's nothin."

CHAPTER 10 DOLLAR

I had already been in Buffalo, New York for a little more than a week, and I was losing my mind. My hormones were so hard to control; those up north chicks love a nigga from down south, and vice versa. Walking through the AIU campus, I had 'Leena on my arm, and I knew I was in trouble. We were checking out her campus, where she would attend school; there were so many exotic women, staring me up, and down, having 'Leena by my side only made things worse. They were really testing her, and I was expecting 'Leena to get ratchet, but she did not, she pretended not to even notice.

I had my gold rimmed Gucci shades covering my eyes. My sixteen solid gold teeth shined, like the 14k gold, 30" iced out Franco chain, with the M&M pendant attached. I had on my gold iced out Jacob wristwatch, and I was draped in COOGI. An orange, red, yellow, and white short sleeve polo shirt, and a pair of blue jeans COOGI shorts. Fresh out of the box Air force 1's was on my feet, the two front pockets of my shorts had a bulge, with $10,000.00 in each of them.

While 'Leena spoked with her school's adviser, I decided to check out the rest of the campus and call to check up on my little nigga Tron. Knowing I was about to leave, I snatched him up to replace me. There were many who could fill my shoes, but I trusted Tron. I gave him a kilo of cocaine, even gave him my trap spot in the projects, and once he set up shop, started to make some money, he was to pay me $15,000.00. But from then on, he was on his own. I showed him how to whip the coke into some good cookies, so I knew he was tearing the projects up.

With Dave knocked out the box I had to find a new plug, and Nico had the best ticket; I started copping from him. Before I left, Nico and I made a wager; he said Tron was not pushing 4 cookies a day, nor did he think he was capable of replacing me; I said he was. Tron was to pay me the $20,000.00 in a week, and when he did Nico was to start selling him work for the same price, he was selling it to me; $20,000.00 a kilo.

"What dat shit hittin' on out dey cuz?" I was cruising through the student union, just checking out the scene. Giving a few smiles and was tempted to try and get a few numbers.

"I'm gettin' it in cousin." Replied Tron, "I got dat for you too."

"Dat what's up. Skyline Nic,' and give it to him. I'm happy you doin' your thing."

"I'm just tryna be like you. You be easy up dey cousin."

"You to my nigga."

"I got no choice." Tron hung up.

Hitting Nico up, I made sure he had my money on the wire, from our bet, then I saw a bookstore with this fine ass chick working the register. Knowing 'Leena needed a few things; I decided I would step in there. Walking into the bookstore, I had a list of things in my mind, I knew I had to get. Those thoughts disappeared when the cashier, and I locked eyes. She was admiring me, and I was locked all the way into her.

She was about 5'10", Dominican, Irish, and Black. Caramel complected, with a 36c-26 46 frame. She had that long, black, and mahogany brown wavy hair; in a ponytail down her back. She had a cute little gap between her front teeth, and they were all pearly white. She also had some small square framed glasses over her eyes. I was digging her style, and she must have been feeling me as well; she was continuously checking me out.

Every few minutes she would look up from her desk, where she was working; she caught me looking each time. Not once did I look away, whenever we locked eyes; she did, while blushing. After grabbing a couple of book bags, the utensils I knew we would need, I headed to the register.

"How are you today?" She asked in her New Jersey accent, as she began to ring up my things.

"I have no reason to complain." I showed the gold grill smile, and she would not stop blushing. "How you doin'?"

"I am great. Thanks for asking. Where are you from?"

I told her I was from Savannah, Ga., and after a few more interrogational questions, her number was going into my cellphone. Paying for our things, I made my exit, with plans of us getting together soon. Walking out of the store, I noticed 'Leena walking into my direction, looking around the student union, oblivious to the fact she had been standing back peeping the whole scene.

"What up mama." I greeted her with my usual charming smile.

"Shit." Getting a bag from me, 'Leena led the way out of the student union. "I'm hungry, and ready to get back to my baby."

"Way, you trying to eat at?" We were walking down the stairs, leading to the parking lot. Approaching my Chevelle, I hit two buttons on my keypad, and the engine started roaring to life.

"We can stop at McDonald's." 'Leena was getting into the passenger seat, and I was hopping into the driver seat; "what you see in her, dat you don't see in me?"

Sticking the key into the ignition, I turned it halfway, then hit the brake. That is when I put the car in drive and began to pull out. "Who are you talkin' 'bout 'Leena?"

"And you gon' play me stupid. Ok Dollah. Da bitch who number you was puttin' in your phone. Dats who da fuck I am talkin' 'bout. What do you see in her, dat you don't see in me?"

"I'm just trying to find some good reefer; she says she know way it's at."

"You know what? If you feel like you have to lie 'bout somethin' so small…. Never mind man. You gon' fuck around and make me do somethin' to you Dollah."

I knew I fucked up, so I started planning ahead, to prevent the same screw-up from happening in the future. I was going to fuck Porsha, the salesclerk; I had to, and wanted to see what the amazon had to offer. As we cruised through the Buffalo streets, I had that Trill, by Bun B, in the tape deck; #11, Hold you down, came on. Turning the volume up a little, I began to sing along.

"If you need Love, I'm lovin.' If you need a thug, I'm thuggin.' If you need a hustler, whatever you need…. Girl Imma hol' you down.

The whole time I sung, I rubbed her thigh. She began to open and close her legs. I knew her pussy was getting wet, but she continued to stare out the passenger window. She was frowned up, with her arms folded across her chest. Knowing she would be over her little tantrum soon, I left her alone, stopped to McDonald's, and headed home.

I pulled into the driveway, of our three beds, two baths, brick home we had downtown. It was on Oxford block, off of E. Ferry & Maine Street. Before I could even get the car in park good, she was out of the car, slamming the door, stomping her way to the front door. Grabbing the bags off the backseat, I hopped out, and headed inside.

"What you done did now?" Queen asked the minute I stepped inside. "Saleena went to da back talkin' really crazy."

Shaking my head, I gave Queen a kiss on her cheek, and looked at Jr.; Queen was feeding him. "Let me go talk to her; I will be back."

From the living room, I went down the hallway on my right, and to the last door on the left. 'Leena was sitting down on the bed when I walked in but jumped to her feet at the sight of me.

"Nigga don't ever try me like dat again." 'Leena slapped the shit out of me, and I took it. Just stared at her like she was crazy. "I know I ain't got a place to go, but I ain't gon' let you fuck me ova. I'll leave and make it on my own first."

"'Leena, you trippin,' I 'on't want dat bitch." Sitting down on the edge of the bed, I just looked up at 'Leena. She was just standing there, with her hands on her hips.

"Whateva nigga." Sucking her teeth, she turned to walk away. Wrapping my hand around her waist, I pulled her back to me. "Let me go." She was trying to get away, but I was not hearing it. Sitting her in my lap, I had my arms wrapped around her, and refused to let her go.

"I promise you I 'on't want dat bitch." I whispered in her ear. "All I want is you. quit trippin."

She was slowly giving in, and once my hands started moving, she finally caved. Gripping her pussy, through her shorts, with one hand, I squeezed one of her breasts with the other. Her hands went over her head, in my hair, and around my neck. She began to grind her ass on my dick, and it shot up like a rocket.

"Hol' up." I unbuckled her shorts; "lock dat doe."

And that was the beginning of many make up after break up sessions.

CHAPTER 11 SALEENA

Everything was a go. I was in school, trying to design myself a line, which will turn many heads. Dollar helped me open my clothing store downtown, and I named it "Finer things." We were doing good on business; Dollar met this guy named Pierre who was actually from New York, and that's who we were getting our clothes from. We were buying everything by the dozen, wholesale for the low.

I attended two classes, every other day; they lasted from 6-10 p.m. One was Fashion Design 101; I was learning how to put the sketches of the outfits I was creating onto the computer, so I could build my portfolio. The other was Basic Business Management; I was in the process of learning how to manage my business. In between working at the store, school, Jr., and that roguish ass Dollar, I felt like I was about to lose my mind.

I was always tired, ripping and running, and I did not get a chance to get much sleep. It was cool though because I was doing something I enjoyed doing. And when I felt myself about to crash, I knew how to put my foot down, and hop in the sack. Take my me time. This particular day was not one of those days; I was going through hell and wanted to blow.

Jr. would not stop screaming, because my phones would not stop ringing. On top of that, the day before was Dollar's birthday, and he has not made his way home yet. I was paranoid. I did not know anything, so I called the hospital, but was told there was not a Dollar listed. I also called the Erie County Jail but got the same results. The first time the phone rung with the private number, I answered because I thought it might have been Dollar, but instead of Dollars voice, I heard moans from both a man and a woman.

I hung up, but the ringing did not stop. It was four in the evening, and the phone has been ringing for the past eight hours. I turned my cellphone off, but that did not do any good, the bitch started calling my house phone. I knew it was a bitch, because she left plenty messages on my answering machine, telling me things I already knew about Dollar. He ain't shit, he is a nasty dirty dick ass nigga; that is just to name a couple of things.

"He gon' wish he were dead or in jail, when I catch his ass." My temper was rising, I continued pacing back, and fourth through the house. Just talking to myself, waiting on Dollar to step through the door. I had finally gotten Jr. to go to sleep, and the phone rang again. I snatched the phone out of the cradle; "what da fuck you keep calling my phone for?"

"Hol' up bitch"

"Bitch?"

"You heard what I said. You need to check that nigga you call your man."

"You know way Dollah at?" That was all I wanted to know.

"I am sorry I do not. He left earlier this morning."

"Oh really. Dat what's up. So how long y'all been fuckin'? Scratch dat, how you got my number?"

"Easy. Your locked in his phone as wifey. I actually thought that was kind of cute. How old are you? Seventeen, eighteen?"

"I'm eighteen."

"You do not have to worry about me trying to take your place, that nigga is not even on my level. I will run circles around his young ass."

For some reason I believed her. That last statement of hers got a little laugh out of me; I was skeptical, however. I wanted to know if they had sex. Before I could ask, she continued.

"And no, we never had sex. He went to sleep drunk on my couch last night. He left early this morning."

That was a relief, but what was up with the moans from the first phone call. "So why you left da messages? And what up wit' da moans I heard ova da phones?"

"Hold up sweetie. That is not my thing, it is child play. I guess Dollar got into one of those little girl's heads."

Just then, the front doorknob turned, and Dollar walked in; "I'm 'bout to get into his head right now. He just walked in."

"Well, I did my part, you take care."

"You too. Bye."

"Bye."

I hung up and met Dollar in the hallway. I wanted to blow, but I took another approach, choosing to be nonchalant about the situation; "you had a good time last night?" I leaned up against one side of the wall, and Dollar leaned against the other side.

"Baby I am sorry, I had a lil too much to drink, and I woke up in dis chick spot dis mornin.' I don't remember nothin."

"It's cool." I walked away, and down the hall to Jr's room. Dollar was on my heels. "I am through worryin' myself 'bout you. I got to go to class, watch Jr."

Grabbing my book bag, I headed out the door, leaving him to wonder. One of my classes were cancelled, so I knew I had a little time to waste; I decided to go get me a drink. Starbucks wasn't as packed as usual; it wasn't packed at all actually. Besides me, there were about ten others. Sitting at the internet bar, I sipped my small vanilla cappuccino, and ate a banana nut muffin.

Trying to send out an email, my laptop went dead. Pulling the adapter out of my book bag, sitting on the floor next to me, I leaned back up, and noticed him walk in the door. Tremaine Mosley: a twenty two year old senior, who also attends AIU, was a true New Yorker. Born, and raised in Brooklyn, NY. Born into a family of hustlers, but chose to take another route at getting money, other than selling drugs.

He wanted to be a producer, had the ear for the music, and loved it with a passion. He stood at 5'7", stocky for his 168 pounds, was black as tar, with a set of some pearly white teeth. He kept the low cut, with the deep waves. He did not do the jewelry thing at all, not even so much as a watch. When it came to the gear though, he was always on point, up to date on the latest, and knew how to rock it.

Stepping into the Starbucks, Tremaine was sporting a pair of blue LRG jeans, a white T-shirt, a long sleeve red, and white LRG button up, with a fresh pair of air force ones, and a white NY fitted cap. It was simple true enough, but he made it look good. Getting back to minding my own business, I plugged the adapter into the wall socket, then my laptop, and once it was started up, I proceeded to send my email out.

"Yo ma, you mind if I sit here?" Tremaine asked, sitting his book bag on the bar.

"Not at all, you good." I was playing calm, but the butterflies in my stomach had me nervous for some reason. I was truly digging this nigga swag, knowing I was not supposed to.

"Yo, you're in my business class." I nodded my head, "yeah, I've been seeing you around, but never had a chance to formally introduce myself. I'm Tremaine."

I shook his hand, told him my name, and we began to converse. One topic led to another, and before either one of us knew it, two hours had passed. We exchanged numbers on some classmate shit, then we headed to class. I could not seem to focus, because my mind was far from school. It was on that upcoming producer, who made everything that came out of his mouth sound so fly. After class, I rode around a little bit, trying to get my thoughts together, then I headed home.

Walking into the living room, the smell of a vanilla candle burning, caught my attention. So Beautiful, by Music Soulchild, was playing through the stereo in the master bedroom at a volume just loud enough to hear walking down the hall. On my way to the master bedroom, I stopped in to check on Jr.; he was laid out in the crib peacefully sleeping. I gave him a kiss on his forehead and headed to the master bedroom.

"What up?" Dollar looked up from his spot on the bed where he was rolling up a blunt of sour diesel reefer, "how was school?"

"It was ok;" I sat down on the edge of the bed and pulled off my navy blue BCBG pullover sweatshirt; "just another day."

"Dat what's up, you wonna hit dis?"

I hit the blunt a couple of times, passed it back, then pulled my navy blue, grey, and white Bo Jackson sneakers off. I grabbed a pair of panties, a bra, and went to take a shower. After getting my night clothes on, I headed back to the room; Dollar was up under the covers, playing to be asleep. I found that out when I slid in bed, and up under the covers. He scooted right up to me and put his hard dick on my ass; I just laid there like a dead duck. He tried everything; kissing on my neck, where my spot was, playing with my breast, and my pussy. He even tried spreading my cheeks, to slide into me; I was not bulging, I had locked my juice box for that night.

"Man fuck dis shit. I'm gon." Throwing the covers off him, he jumped out of bed mumbling.

"Leave den nigga. I don't care." I also jumped out of bed, and as he was getting dressed, I was pulling clothes off hangers in the closet. Throwing them at him, I continued; "take all your shit wit' you. And when your dirty dick ass leave, you bet not come back!"

Dollar pulled a Red Monkey shirt over his head and stared into my eyes. "Dats how you feel?" I just rolled my eyes, then he pulled a gym bag from under the bed and began to stuff it with clothes. Sitting down on the edge of the bed, I just watched him pack. I wanted to stop him, but I could not. Walking out of the bedroom, he turned around, looked at me, shook his head from side to side, and left. That's when I broke down and started crying. I cried for about an hour, before I finally fell asleep.

CHAPTER 12 DOLLAR

Shit was going as planned, other than every other month feuds between 'Leena, and I. True, it was mainly my fault, I couldn't control my dog ass ways. I tried, but I had a major thing for older women, and they were messing my head up. I met this one chick named Dianna, who was 32, with two jobs, three degrees, and still going to school. Owned a three-bedroom town house, an old school 'Lac, and a new School 'Lac. She had no kids, standing 5'9", and was sexy like Stacy Dash; German, and treated me like I was gold.

That chick was crazy and wanted me to give her all my time. She wanted me there every night, even wanted to marry me; we have not even known each other three months. It should have been a red flag somewhere in the play, but shit I got to be honest, the pussy, and her head was soooo good I could not see past it. Not to forget the couple stacks a week she was giving me, the keys to the house, and cars. She even threw the old school 'Lac in the game and gave it to me.

Dr. Jekyll turned into Mrs. Hyde when I left her ass alone. She turned into a real stalker. Whenever I stepped out of the house, she was somewhere around. She tried to fight 'Leena when she saw us together, she even tried to run me over with her car. She threw me all the way out of my square with that crazy shit.

On the school tip, I was doing my thing; mostly B's, with a couple of A's, and I was improving my b-ball skills. I was bringing that street ball to the court, under the whistle, and I was going hard in the paint; aggressive. Not too many people could handle me when it came to that ball, nor when it came to my hustle. I had the campus on smash! Nico was plugging me in with the coke, the pills, and the reefer for a good ticket; $20,000.00 got me a block, ten pounds of reefer, and 1000 pills.

I was killing their ass, tow truck style; every delivery I got a new old school and tricked it out. Rode them for a few weeks, then put them on the market. After no one bought the first two, I decided to stop trying to sell them, and just put them in storage. Since I started hustling around on the campus, I had flipped six whips; that is six different trips, and from each trip, I profited $35,000.00. Young, and enjoying life, I had nothing to complain about.

There were a lot of envious niggas out there, but I never expected those niggas to try, and knock me out the box the way they did. I thought one of those haters would try to rob me, so I kept my forty even when I was shitting on the toilet. Thought they would tell the people on me, so I did not keep anything at home; everything was locked away in storage with no ties to me. There was one person at the storage I dealt with, and after a little hush money, no ID was needed.

After months of nonstop going to school, hustling, and grinding, I was excited to hear Money Go Getters Ent. was bringing Young Jeezy, Plies, TI, and Keyshia Cole to club Infinity. I decided to bring my whips out. Marcus was attending Miami university, but one call and he came up, with his slut for a girl Kim on his side. Tron even came to kick it with me; he brought about six strapped goons from the projects, and from the looks of things, he was the Boss Man. When I saw that, I laughed, thinking back to when we use to tell

Dave we wanted to be just like him.

We hit the mall and did a little shopping; that is where I copped my COOGI outfit from. When I saw it in the window, I had to have it. Some black COOGI jeans, with COOGI going down the right pants leg in chestnut brown, tan, and white. A black, chestnut brown, tan, and white COOGI sweater with the skully to match. The chestnut brown ostrich print COOGI sport boots, blended well with the chestnut brown ostrich print leather jacket, also by COOGI. My whole squad was up to par; jewelry game was sick, whip game was sick, and I pulled all of them out for the occasion.

I was pushing the Benz, 'Leena's Benz; it was sprayed black, with the peanut butter guts, and some 22" black Asanti rims. When we pulled into the parking lot of club Infinity, all eyes were on us. The regular parking spaces were to the left, when we entered the driveway, the humongous club was to the right. We rode through the parking lot, past the club, and to the dead end. Turning around, we parked in a vertical line in front of the parallel parked cars, facing the front of the club; our trunks were going crazy, and our candy were wet like it just got done raining. We were truly putting on a show.

"Yo son you can't park here." Some clown said as he walked over to where we were parked. I shut him up really quick.

"Oh, cousin we gon' park here." Hopping out, my team began to hop out too. Pulling a dope boy knot of money from my pants pocket, I continued. "What it's gon' cost?"

Looking from the knot to the cars, to my team, he looked back at me with a smile; "five hundred a car."

There were eight cars; giving him the $4,000.00, we entered the club. There was a line stretched out the length of the club in the front; we walked straight in the front door. No pat down, or anything. Stepping in the door, there was a room the size of a walk-in closet. To the left was a glass window, with a glass double door next to it. We stepped through the doors, paid the cashier, who was posted at the counter on our left, then we burst through the double doors, and into the club.

It was going down. There was a small bar to the left, the length of the wall; at the end was a set of spiral stairs, leading up to the VIP floor. To the right, was a long bar; it was the length of the wall, where another set of spiral stairs were. It also led up to the VIP floor. Straight ahead was the stage; there were a set of spiral stairs in the far-right corner, leading up to the DJ booth. Club Infinity was packed, people were everywhere. The bar, the stage, the big ass dance floor, where people were getting their groove on to the latest jams, bumping through the dozen speakers scattered out through the club.

We made a quick stop at the bar, and tore it down, then we headed to the VIP. I paid the guy at the bottom of the stairs $5,500.00, for us all to go up, and once we made it upstairs, we found a couple of booths. The VIP was in the shape of a rectangle. On the back wall, was a set of private booths sectioned off by a velvet curtain; in the middle of the floor, was a circular bar. Just so happen, we were able to get two booths, in the middle, behind the bar.

Bottles started popping, blunts got rolled, and we started our night. While everybody was having fun, I was thinking on ways of making more money; well other spots to set up shop. Right up the street from my house, there is a store called quick stop, and behind it is an apartment complex, which is a decent size. I would not call it the projects, but it was close to it, and according to the little chick I met who stays there, there is plenty of money being made there through crack. I said I was not going to fuck around to close to home, but I was becoming money hungry, I wanted it all, and planned to propose a deal to Tron about running the operation.

"Baby come on. Dance wit' me." 'Leena was on her feet, pulling my arm.

I was not into the dancing thing, but all I had to do with 'Leena is stand there and bob my head. She did the rest. I got up and followed her over to the front of the VIP, where the balcony was. I love your girl, by the dream was blaring through the speakers; 'Leena was rocking her hips from side to side, while I gripped one of those hips with one hand and held on to my cup with the other. Her ass was on my dick, and I was beginning to stretch out, but not because of what she was doing; I spotted Porsha in the crowd looking in my direction, winding for me. Catching me looking, she smiled then turned away.

'Leena kept me on the dance for about thirty minutes. When the show started, I decided to take a breath, and roll up. Keyshia Cole started with that Remember; 'Leena grinded my dick to that. Plies did his Bust it baby, then they did plies' Number one fan, together. Young Jeezy did several numbers, and so did TI. While TI was finishing his Whatever you like, track, we headed to the entrance.

Stepping out the club, I noticed one of my cars were gone. Looking around, I was determined to find the clown I paid the money to. Spotting him chopping it up with a little chick, I made my way over to him.

"Yo what's up son." He had this devious smile on his face.

I hit first and asked the question later; I punched him dead in the mouth, dropping him to his knees. I kicked him in his stomach, and face continuously, asking numerous times; "way my car at?"

He did not respond, so I kept kicking him, until Marcus pulled me off him. He walked me over to 'Leena's Benz, and once I was in the passenger seat, I realized how drunk I was. I just kept mumbling to myself. Wanting to get out and beat him some more. Might have done it, if 'Leena would have waited a few more minutes to pull out. But she pulled out immediately.

"Are you goin' to report it stolen?" 'Leena was swerving in and out of traffic, in route to the interstate, so we could head home.

"Man, fuck dat car!" Rolling a blunt of sour diesel, I continued mumbling to myself, then relaxed once I put fire to it.

"Ok. So, you beat his ass for what?"

"For stealin' from me. Nobody steals from me and get away wit' it."

'Leena did not bother to respond, she turned the radio up, and let that Beyoncé cd ride; by the time we made it home, let the babysitter go home, and get ourselves situated, it was damn near 4:00 a.m. I fucked 'Leena to sleep, then laid there holding her for about thirty minutes thinking before I fell asleep. Every day, throughout the whole weekend, it was the same thing; I paid for it all that Monday morning.

Not only did I have a massive headache, and a hangover, I had practice 7:45 that morning. We were in the middle of bounce passing, and every time the ball bounced, my head pounded. But I was not about to give in. In the middle of our scrimmage game, coach called me to the sideline, and told me the student advisor wanted to see me. I headed halfway across the campus to his office, to find out why he wanted to see me. The minute I stepped in, I knew I was in some shit.

"Sit down." I sat down in the chair, in front of his desk, and he continued; "I have heard quite a few things about you. Some may be true, and some may not be. I will leave it for you to answer. Are you selling any kind of narcotics at all on the school premises?"

"All I do is play ball."

"That's good to know." He pulled a urinalysis cup from one of the drawers on his desk and sat it down on top of the desk. "So, you won't have a problem passing this will you?"

I thought about it for a second, wanted to lie, but said, "I won't be able to pass dat dough. I smoke reefer."

"I like your honesty Keven, but drugs are one of those things we cannot tolerate. I am going to have to ask you to sign out of school, or we are going to have to put you out. What is it going to be?"

The whole ride to the house, I was trying to figure out how I was going to break the news to 'Leena. When I pulled into the driveway, I already had a grand plan that would be beneficial for the both of us. Stepping inside, I made my way to the back of the house, and to the master bedroom. 'Leena was lying on her back, in the bed, holding Jr. in the air. He had his arms, along with his legs spread wide, pretending to fly.

"What up baby. Why you back so early?" She never looked my way. She was busy smiling at Jr.

"I had to sign out of school." Taking a seat on the edge of the bed, 'Leena sat Jr. down on the bed, and I smiled as he crawled to me.

"Baby for what?"

"Dey wanted me to piss in uh cup, but I tol' Mr. Freeman I smoke. He said its either sign out, or dey gon' put me out."

"Ok. So, what are we going to do now?"

"You gon' keep doin' what you are doin', and I'm 'bout to go to Tennessee."

"And leave us here alone. No deal. We are comin' too."

"You need to finish school and run da store."

"I will find somebody to run da store, and I will find somethin' I like down dey."

"You sure?"

"Yep."

"Ok den. Tennessee, we go. Let's take uh trip to find us a house."

CHAPTER 13 SALEENA

I didn't know how bad I had messed up until after I signed out of school and moved to Tennessee with Dollar. He copped us a nice three bedroom, two bath brick home; it was out in Nashville Tennessee. That's where I spent most of my time; I was home with Jr. I didn't get into Tennessee State, and there wasn't anything at Tennessee Tech I wanted to major in; I wasn't about to work, so I kicked back, took care of Jr., as well as our home. When we first made it to Ten a key, everything was good; the fighting between Dollar, and I were to a minimum, and we were on good terms. After a while though, the nigga got on some more shit.

He became verbally abusive; everything that came out of his mouth was some negative shit. 'You need to get off your ass, you are falling off, gettin' fat. You ain't got shit goin' for yourself. I don't know why I fuck wit' your lazy ass.' Things like that. It was only the beginning; he started staying away from home two, three nights at a time, without so much as a courtesy call. I wasn't bothering to call him either; I spent those nights crying over the phone, to Tremaine; he was a good listener.

Just thinking about Tremaine, has me blushing. But anyway, I was trying my hardest to keep Dollar happy. I worked out daily, to keep my body tight. I kept his stomach full, and his nut sack empty, but that wasn't good enough to keep him home. At the time I didn't know what was needed to be done. We eventually quit talking to one another, well he quit talking to me; whenever I spoke to him, it was like I was talking to myself.

Deep down, I knew Dollar had someone else. Though I couldn't prove it, my intuition let me know, but clarity is what I needed to confront his ass. One night Dollar came home drunk, and high after a whole week. I played it all the way cool, like I didn't give a damn. Thinking I was asleep, he put all three of his phones on the nightstand, then went to take a shower; determined to find something, I started checking his phones.

I went through his text messages, call logs, the pictures, but I came up with nothing incriminating. Sitting on the edge of the bed, I thought about my next move; I headed to the bathroom.

"Baby dat's you?" Dollar asked reaching his arm around the shower curtain to grab his 40 Caliber; it was sitting on the back of the toilet.

"Yea." Stepping in, I took my seat on the toilet; "I got to use da bathroom." He continued to bathe, and I began checking through the pockets of his Red Monkey jean shorts, sitting on the floor. "Way you been?"

"In da trap." I found a huge knot of money, in each of his short's pocket, but nothing else. No condoms, no numbers, nothing.

I wiped myself, flushed the toilet, and after washing my hands I headed back into the room. Dollars phone screen had lit up, so I sat down on the bed, and grabbed it from the nightstand. There was a new text message just came in. I opened it up and read it.

I can't wait to see you this weekend. I should be arriving Friday, between 12:00 and 1:00. Stay sweet.

"Oh really?" The number wasn't saved in his phone, but I was determined to find out who she was. I wanted to call back but decided against it; I sat the phone back down where it was and sat there for a minute thinking.

Seeing Dollar step into the room, it took everything I had inside of me not to snap. I wanted to jump on him. I just stared at him, while he got himself together for bed, wondering what I was going to do to him, and his bitch when I caught them together. Friday, between 12:00, and 1:00.

Waking up to the sound of Dollar breathing on my neck, the warmth of his lips on my cheek, the touch of his fingers on my skin, and the feel of his heart beating with mine, always excited me. When Friday arrived, I wasn't fazed by none of that. I eased out of bed, and after handling my womanly duties, I went to see about Jr.

"What you doin' lil man?" When I stepped into Jr. room, there were clothes everywhere on the floor, and he was walking around in a circle, trying to pull a shirt over his head. It seemed to be stuck around his face; I attempted to help; "come 'ere."

"I ju it ma!" He snatched away, and within seconds, he had the shirt over his head. I just stood back smiling at his little mannish ass. "See?!"

"Yea I see." I snatched him off the ground, and held him high up in the air, then dropped him on the bed, and tickled his stomach. "Snatch away from me again and see what I do to you."

"Otay!!!" He couldn't control his laughter, and I continued to tickle him.

"What you in here doin' to my son?" Dollar walked into the room and snatched Jr. into his arms.

"We just coolin." I took a seat on the edge of Jr's bed, and Dollar sat down next to me. Jr. stood in Dollar's lap, tugging on his dreadlocks.

"Yea dada we jus' coo 'in."

"Baby go get dressed." Dollar put Jr. on the ground, "and you clean up dis damn room."

"Way, we goin'?" I wanted to know.

"Jus' go get dressed and let me know when you ready to go."

"Aight."

We ended up at IHOP, eating breakfast. I had the Roody Toody Fresh 'N Fruity, and the few bites I did eat was good. I didn't have much of an appetite, my mind was elsewhere. Between 12:00, and 1:00. I continued to check my lady Movado wristwatch, because I was expecting Dollar to ditch us, so he could get up with his girl on the side. Dollar caught me off guard by where he took us next. The Range Rover dealership, out in Memphis Tennessee.

When we pulled into the dealership, and Dollar hopped out, I sat there thinking he was there to see someone. That is until he walked around to my side of the Benz, and opened my door; he helped me, then Jr. out. Telling me to choose one, had me staring at him like he was crazy; then the half smile that always makes me melt came. I started scanning the lot. There were Range Rovers everywhere; many different years, makes, models, and colors.

An all-white Range Rover Sport, with jet black tinted windows, and some white 22" rims, caught my attention. I headed over in the direction of where it was with Dollar, and Jr. on my heels. Trying to see through the windows, a salesman walked up, and unlocked the driver door. The moment I sat in the driver seat, I knew it was the one I wanted. Hopping out of the black leather bucket seat, I told Dollar it was the one I wanted.

Dollar didn't ask the price. He left us there posted at the SUV, while he grabbed a duffel bag from out of the trunk of the Benz. When he made his way back over, Dollar gave the bag to the salesman, told him to give me the paperwork, then told me he'll meet me at the mall; he had to check on one of his spots. I didn't bother to protest, I was getting a new car, and I was going shopping.

After taking care of the paperwork, I put Jr. in the backseat, and we pulled out. I called Dollar to let him know we were leaving, but he didn't answer the phone. That's when my mind got back on track, and I checked my watch. It was a quarter till 1:00, and that's when I realized I got tricked.

I headed to the mall anyway. After thirty minutes of walking around K B Toys store, behind Jr, Dollar finally called to say he was pulling in. He gave me some lame excuse about one of his workers stealing from the stash, and I ate it up knowing if I blew, I would never get to the bottom of what other bitch he was fucking. Instead, I made him spend his money.

He blew a quick eight stacks on us, then he followed us home. While I was getting Jr. out, Dollar went on inside with most of the bags. Jr. was knocked out, so I carried him to his room, and laid him down, then headed to the master bedroom. Stepping through the threshold, I noticed Dollar was packing; not just a carry-on bag, but this nigga was packing suit cases.

Wanting to know what the hell was going on, I asked; "what's goin' on? Way, you goin'?" I slowly made my way over to the bed to take a seat.

"Who da fuck is Tremaine, Saleena?" Dollar looked up from the spot on the floor, where he'd been kneeling.

Jumping to my feet, I tried to plead my case. Not knowing how much he really knew; I knew I had to be straight up with Dollar. With my hands on my hip, I stared into Dollars eyes, and said, "I met him when I was in school, he was in one uh my classes."

"You fucked him?"

"What?! Hell no!! Who tol' you some shit like dat?"

"One uh my lil homies up North say he broadcasting how he smashed you."

I thought back to the night I almost slipped up and gave in to Tremaine. Dollar, and I were beefing as usual; I got drunk, and ended up at Tremaine's spot, pillow talking. He had a slick tongue, was saying all the right things, while at the same time, his hands were touching the right spots, and his lips were all over my skin. He ended up giving me some good head, but that's as far as it went. When he climbed on top of me, and was trying to penetrate, I stopped him; Dollar popped into my mind, and I left.

"Baby I swear nothin' happened between us." I was to the point of ears; I didn't want to lose Dollar. Other than my son, shit he was all I had.

Sitting down on the bed next to me, Dollar ran his hand through his dreadlocks, and dry washed his face. Letting out a muffled sigh, he said; "Listen 'Leena, I love you, but I can't do dis no more."

"Do what? I tol' you I ain't fuck him."

"Well, what did happen?"

I broke down, and told him what went down between Tremaine, and I. He let it be known, he didn't know anything other then what I told him, and how he found Tremaine's number in my phone. He tricked me into telling on myself, and after chumping me off, he grabbed his things, and left. I just sat there on the bed crying; I knew there was more to why Dollar left, had to be another woman, with more to offer than I had. Sad, and depressed, I once again cried myself to sleep.

CHAPTER 14 DOLLAR

It hurt me more than anything to walk out on 'Leena, but shit it is what it is. I got tired of babysitting her grown ass. I did the best I could to help her. I got her in school, opened a business for her, that I ended up running from another state. I gave her any, and everything she needed. I guess that was probably part of the problem, babying her.

On the flip side, I was attending Tennessee state university, and I was on an academic scholarship. Being the first college, who wanted me to attend their school, they gladly accepted me. The things I learned at the Spike Air academy, in New York, they came in handy, and I quickly became the man on campus. I enrolled in the early part of January, and because of my stats, I took a starting position on the basketball team, as a power forward.

Averaging twenty points, nine rebounds, and twelve assist per game, I had agents calling my phone left, and right. During the March Madness, coach Graham, the Atlanta Hawks head coach, came and personally asked me to join their team. I declined; I was majoring in business management and wanted to finish school first. Getting my degree was something I dedicated myself to get; I needed something to fall back on, in case something was to happen while playing ball. I was no longer touching the dope, but I was still seeing the dope money though.

Tron, and his little thugs opened shop in New York; they were in the apartments I was scoping out before I left, and they were tearing it up with that crack. They were getting money, and the end of the month, Tron broke me off. I had money stashed everywhere; Queen spot, 'Leena spot, Porsha spot, and I'm not talking about five and ten grand. More like one fifty or better; I wasn't in the millionaire spot, I spent unnecessary money on unnecessary things I know I didn't need. But I was living the life of the Boss I considered myself to be.

I copped me a little two bedroom, two bath condo out in Knoxville, Ten, and decked it out. Everything white, and black, like DMX spot was on Belly. I bought the most expensive things too; I blew about $30,000.00 just to get the inside done to my liking. Ostrich skinned leather sofas, 72" plasma screens in both rooms, Versace bedroom sets, and I even through cameras up. My pad was on point and ducked off; a couple hours away from the college, and I liked it that way.

No one knew where I stayed, other than Queen, and my lady Porsha. She spent more time there, than her own spot, and I didn't mind. She was my motivator, motivated me to want more out of life, motivated me to want to do better. She graduated from AIU, with a bachelor's in accounting, and got a job working for Medicare, as an accountant. She was working in New York, then transferred to the branch in Tennessee, just to be near me.

She had her own house, own car, no kids, and she knew all there was to know about 'Leena. She knew we could get back together at any time, but she knew how to play her position, and played it well. I wasn't in Love with her, but I had much love for her. Not only did she suck me good, and fuck me great, she hit me with much knowledge, and she took time getting to know Jr. For a twenty-four-year-old, Porsha had that grown & sexy thing on smash; straight from the hood, but knew when to be hood, and when to be a lady.

I even began to let our relationship go public, and she stayed on my arm. My nigga Marcus came through on me with Kim one weekend, and they met Porsha; the four of us went out to eat, then Kim shot off to meet up with 'Leena. Marcus, and I hit the club. I have no idea what Kim told 'Leena, but whatever it was, 'Leena was slowly getting herself together. She got herself in school, majoring in criminal justice, wanting to be a detective. She even got a job at the Blount County jail, as a jailer.

I was truly happy for her, and let it be known. At least twice a week, I pulled up and took them out. Sometimes its dinner, sometimes it's a movie. When the James E. Straights moving carnival hit Knoxville, I had to take my little man. Parking my Tahoe in her driveway, we climbed into 'Leena's Range, and headed out.

It was extremely packed, almost to the point of bumping into each other, but we managed to get around ok. Jr. was happy, and sad at the same time. There were several rides he watched the big kids get on, wanted to get on, but he was too small. I brightened up his day though, by buying him all the candy, and sweets he wanted. My little ace ate a candy apple, cotton candy, most of my funnel cake, and a few other snacks.

When Jr. locked eyes on this big ass lion bear, posted up on the Long-Range rack of bears, he pointed, and 'Leena tried to win him one. She couldn't shoot for nothing. $20.00, thirty shots; still no bear, and that damn dread, who was running the booth wasn't helping. He was talking more shit than a little bit.

"Yuh nah hit guh." His Jamaican accent, blowing through the bullhorn, caught those who were passing by attention; not to forget the crazy things he was saying. "Two dollah, tree shot." Whenever 'Leena missed, he yelled "blose!" Then he would burst into laughter. "Yuh feed me when yuh shoot. One time more."

"Damn I can't hit dis shit!" 'Leena gave me her little sad face and handed me the ball. "Get my money back."

"Wah? Yuh tink yuh shoot betta?" Asked the dread. "Yuh try."

At first, I just shot the ball, thinking it was a normal rim, like one from the gym, and I lost $20.00. Dread kept talking trash, and as I learned what kind of rim it was, I continued to lose money. When I realized it was a double rim, like the ones in the projects, and the shot was an oval shot, I decided to throw the bait out there, and see if the dread would bite.

Setting myself to shoot, I brought the ball back down, and turned to look at him. "You talk a lot of shit dread, give me a head up. First one to twenty-five; five racks."

"Yuh on bredren." Dread smiled, showing his mouth full of gold teeth; setting up at the booth next to me, he looked at me at continued; "fie tousand nuttin. Yuh shoot."

I popped it off, making shot, after shot. Dread was with me though; for every shot I made, he made one. Everybody stopped to watch, and from the murmuring behind us, they seemed entertained. Somehow, I missed a basket, and he took off, making it to twenty-five before me.

"Bet it back," I pulled my $10,000.00 knot out of my pants pocket and slapped it in his hand. "Dat's ten."

He smiled, but said nothing; setting up to shoot, we took off. We were flowing on the same rhythm, shot after shot, then he missed. Wanting to keep him in the game, I missed one, and we were back on track. We were in our last few shots, when I realized he was a second ahead of me. Shooting the ball with my right hand, I threw my left hand over his face. He laughed as he bobbed his head around my hand, to hit the shot. He beat me to twenty-five again.

"Woo." Dread sang, as he counted his money out. Reaching $5,000.00, he tried giving it back to me; I closed his hand around it. He looked me up, and down then leaned against his booth. "Weh yuh from bredren?"

"I'm from Savannah, but I'm goin' to TSU. Dey call me Dollah."

"Yeah, me know me see yuh on dey tube. Nice. Me Wayne." He

pulled a business card from his back pocket and gave it to me. "Yuh come tuh di battam, gimme call." Looking down at Jr., who was standing at my side, not missing anything, Wayne said, "Wah yuh see yuh wa? Mi wi gi tuh yuh."

"Die one!" Jr. was pointing at the lion teddy bear.

"Wah one?" Wayne opened the door to the trailer, sitting next to the booth.

"Die one!" he pointed at the lion bear again but wouldn't move from by my leg. I told him to go and get his bear; getting the one he wanted, he ran back over to us yelling; "I got cat! I got cat!"

"I see dat." That was 'Leena. "I like your lion."

I chunked up the deuces at Wayne, and he nodded his head up, and down, as he continued to smile. 'Leena said she was tired, so we left. By the time we made it to 'Leena's house, Jr. was knocked out in the back seat. Carrying him inside, I put him in bed, and when I laid him down, he reached out for me. I made sure he was able to grab a hold of me, and once he turned on his side to get comfortable, he was back to sleep, and I slipped away.

Walking into the master bedroom, my dick jumped; 'Leena was heading to the bathroom naked. I was on my way there as well, undressing as I made my way. By the time I reached the door of the bathroom, my dick was dangling in the wind. 'Leena grabbed my hand, and slightly pulled me into the stand-up shower. Hot water from the shower head sprinkled down over us, as we embraced one another, letting our tongues have a fight.

Her hands started moving, touching me all over. Grabbing one of her legs, I wrapped it around my waist, then gripped her pussy from the back with the same hand. Jumping off her right leg, she locked it with her left leg, around my waist. Holding her up with my forearm, I began to slowly finger fuck her from the back. Running her hands through my dreadlocks, she was grinding against my chiseled chest. Gripping both ass cheeks, I lifted her up, bringing her pussy lips to my lips, then I went to work on her pussy.

Sucking on her clit, I slid one of my middle fingers in her ass; sliding it in, then pulling it out had her moaning, grabbing ahold of me, and seeming not to want to let go. 'Leena tried climbing over my head, I had her feeling so good. But I spared her the pleasure she was expecting until later. Wanting to feel her insides, I brought her back down, so she could cover my rock-hard dick. She started riding my dick, and she was throwing that pussy at me; I was throwing my dick right back at her.

Climaxing, 'Leena continued grinding up, and down on my dick. Gripping my dick with her muscles, she was trying to break me, and I was trying to buck, but she was riding like a true cowgirl. I came all inside of 'Leena, and as I started going soft, she slid down my body, to her knees. Looking at my dick, she grabbed it, and licked the underside of it; the length of it. Up, and down, slowly stroking it back to life as she did. Reaching my balls, she sucked on one, then the other.

She knew just what needed to be done to turn me on, and she was doing so. Stroking my dick with one hand, while playing with one of my balls with her free hand and sucking on my other ball. I had a hand full of her micro braided hair, wrapped up around my wrist, and was holding it tight.

"Damn girl." I moaned, my dick jerked, and I tried to pull away.

'Leena wouldn't let go at first. But when she did, she bent over, reached down, and touched her toes. Reaching back, she spread her ass cheeks so she could bust her pussy open for me. I slid my steel hard dick inside of her pussy, and slow stroked 'Leena as I gripped her hips.

"Ooooh baby." 'Leena was grinding her ass on my dick, with her hands over my head, pulling my dreadlocks; "make me cum on dat dick."

Picking up my rhythm, little by little, I was hitting rock bottom with every stroke. Reaching out to place her hands on the shower wall, she went stiff; started climaxing. The way she was working her pussy muscles, I could feel my cum rising to the top, and I tried to hold it. I couldn't, I started to cum, and 'Leena was milking every drop of semen that shot out of my dick.

'Leena fell forward; I grabbed her waist, pulled her into my arms, and together we dropped down to a sitting position. Grabbing a rag, and a bar of soap, I began to bathe 'Leena. Grabbing a rag, she did the same. Once we were both lathered up, we stood so we could rinse off. Pulling down the detachable shower head, I slowly rinsed 'Leena off.

After bathing each other once more, we stepped out of the shower, and walked over to the bed, dripping wet. I laid down on the bed, and she straddled me. Kissing my face, she slow grinded my dick. Tired of being teased, my dick slid into 'Leena; I squeezed her hips, as she slowly began to ride my dick.

Thrusting my dick up into 'Leena, I was matching her rhythm. "Oh shit." She moaned. "Right dey baby. Right dey."

She tried taking control of the situation, but I had her hips in the palm of my hands. 'Leena's legs began to shake, but she was going hard in the paint. She continued to ride me, and I was slowly getting weak. Sensing it, 'Leena placed her hands on my chest, and went crazy on my dick. Circles, up, and down; the whole time she worked her pussy muscles. I came inside of 'Leena.

She collapsed and fell down on top of me. My dick was still inside of her pussy. Within minutes we were both asleep in each other's arms.

CHAPTER 15 SALEENA

Dollar leaving was a blessing, and a curse. I figured out what needed to be done and did it. I enrolled myself into Tennessee Technical institute in Nashville, Tennessee. My major was in criminal justice, and I was learning to become a detective. I also got myself a job at the Blount County Jail, as a jailer. Seeing so many different types of men, who tried spitting game at me, I stayed horny; but I only wanted Dollar, and wasn't giving up my goodies to anyone.

I copped myself a bullet, with some extra batteries, and I played with my pussy almost every damn night. I had these videos in my phone, Dollar and I recorded, and I used those to help get myself off. It became a part of my daily routine, and even though Dollar wasn't stopping by too often, I wasn't complaining. I spent my time doing things needed to be done, like raising Jr. and studying my notes from class. I was trying to get myself together and knew the only person who could do that was me.

I knew about Porsha; Kim told me everything; even showed me a picture of the chick in her cellphone. She was the same chick Dollar was talking to in the bookstore, when I started AIU. The one he claimed was going to help him get some reefer. Officially he wasn't my man anymore, so I couldn't get mad. Instead, I enjoyed the time we did spend together, as I continued to elevate myself. In my mind, she was just filling in for me, and once I got myself together, she would be gone.

The chance I was waiting on, finally came; Dollars 21st birthday. He was throwing a big ass party at Club Tenn, and I was determined to win his Love. I hit the mall, bought this nice ass mini dress, with some bad ass pumps to match. The mini dress was all black, with the studded strap action; it hugged my breast, my hips, and my ass just right. The black Manolo pumps set it off; they stopped at the top on my calves, and were open toed, showing my pedicured toes.

Throwing on my black Louis V belt, I slid some iced out slim hoop earrings in my ear. Put my gold rope chain, with a medallion charm around my neck, and I slid my Louis V sunglasses over my eyes. Grabbing my Louis Vuitton pouch, I was ready to go. Jr. was already gone with the babysitter, so the only thing I was waiting on, was Kim to get ready. Then it was time to step out.

Club Tenn was thick that night. People of many nationalities were dressed to impress, and the parking lot across the street from the club, was congested with a mixture of old schools, and new schools. We were in my Range, and after finding a safe parking spot, we pulled the mirrors down to check our makeup.

"Girl, you see dat nigga?" Kim asked, as she pointed to a baller who was stepping out of a 2009 Aston Martin. "Marcus might be mad tonight."

"Uhm." That nigga was nowhere in my mind; I didn't even bother to see who she was pointing at. I was applying lip-gloss to my lips. "I see him."

"Bitch you weren't even looking. Dat nigga Dollah got you fucked up."

"Hell, yea he does." I fell back into my seat and thought just how bad he did have my mind messed up. I smiled, then looked at Kim. "I'm 'bout to go and get my man."

"Shit let's go!"

Stepping through a set of double glass doors, we entered the foyer. The VIP section could be seen through a glass window on the wall to the left. It was still early, but the VIP was already packed. After being scanned by a metal detector, we stepped through another set of glass doors, and into the club. Straight ahead was the rectangular bar, and that's where we got our drinks from. I had a glass of Nuevo, and Kim had a Long Island Iced Tea.

We stood posted at the bar, rocking our hips to The Boss, by Rick Ross featuring T-Pain; we decided to scope out the scene, before making any moves. I can't tell you what Kim was looking for, but I was trying to find Dollar. Searching through the crowd of people on the dance floor, the stage, and the VIP that took up damn near the whole left side of the club, I didn't see him. Immediately I became depressed; leaning my back up against the bar, I used the straw in my drink to stir it up. Kim peeped my move.

"Oh no bitch. Not tonight. Not on my watch." Kim grabbed my hand and began to lead me through the crowd. "Come on, I got chu."

Kim led us through the pack of wolves, to the other side of the club, and to the VIP entrance. Kim paid the bouncer $50.00 to open the velvet rope, then he let us through. When we stepped up the few steps, and entered the VIP, there were two directions we could go; left, or right. To the left, was where the dozen or more booths were lined up, and to the right, was the VIP dance floor with the bar all the way at the end. We went to get us a booth.

Kim pulled a blunt, and a sack of reefer from her bag; after rolling it, she passed it, along with a lighter to me. Putting fire to it, I inhaled it a few good times, and started to relax. As Kim's eyes started to roam the club, so did mine. There were many attractive dudes throughout the club, but none of them really caught my attention. I caught several looking in my direction smiling, and I gave them a friendly smile, but continued to let my eyes roam the room.

One nigga I smiled at, must've taken it as an invitation; he walked across the club, and to the VIP. He had his homeboy with him, and they were both clean, but neither was my type. They were both well over 6', big as hell, and RED; a major turn off for me. When they approached our table, I was about to dismiss their ass really quick, but Kim saw my mouth open, and she slapped my knee under the table. I decided to let it do what it do.

"How are you ladies doing today? I'm Kareem." He reached out for me to shake his hand, and I did. "And this my man Travis. Mind if we sit down?"

"Nah we don't mind." Kim blurted out, smiling at Travis. "I'm Michelle and dis my sister Brandy."

"Oh ok." Kareem sat next to me, and Travis sat next to Kim. "So where are y'all from? If you don't mind me asking."

"Georgia. We attend Tennessee Tech."

I was nowhere in that conversation. The whole time Kim talked for us; I was busy looking around the club. If Big Red thought he was getting some play from me, he was out of his mind. Kim on the other hand, was giving Travis all her attention. They were laughing and shit, at jokes I didn't find too funny at all. Wanting to get away from that little bunch, I decided to get another drink.

Looking over at Kim, I said; "I'm 'bout to hit dis bar. You want somethin'?"

"Yeah. Get me a long island."

Travis looked at Kareem, who slid out the booth, to let me out; he said; "grab a bottle of Patron. I got you."

I knew what that meant. Rolling my eyes, I headed to the bar.

Kareem was right behind me, and when the crowd on the VIP dance floor saw him, they parted like the red sea. We placed our orders, and I leaned up against the bar to wait for the bartender to make my drinks. Kareem leaned against the bar next to me.

"Can I ask you a question?" Kareem asked.

"I'm listenin'." I didn't bother to even look in his direction.

"Why your fine ass looking so mean?"

"Lookin' so mean? Dis my happy face."

"Well, I would love to see how you look, when you get mad." I rolled my eyes, not even pondering on a response.

I grabbed our drinks, he grabbed their bottle, and we headed back to the booth. As we were sitting down, I noticed him walk in, Dollar, and his click. My pussy instantly got wet, just from looking at him. That nigga Dollar was looking damn good in that black linen fit, with the black Ostrich square toes to match. His dreads were pulled back into a real neat ponytail, his watch, bracelet, pinky ring, and the two chains around his neck glistened as the strobe lights hit them. I was so caught up, I forgot where I was sitting, and who I was sitting with.

"Oh, that's why I've been getting the cold shoulder."

My mind got right quick; I looked at Kareem, and said, "listen, you seem like cool people and all," I looked around, and them niggas were walking into the VIP. Dollar, and I locked eyes; I broke away, and continued with telling Kareem what was on my mind. "But y'all have to find some way else to sit."

"Yep." Kim, and Marcus were having a stare down as they moved toward our booth.

"Understood. I'll catch you later." Kareem stood to leave, Travis did too.

"Yea. Later." They quickly walked away.

"Damn you couldn't wait on me to start da party?" Marcus bent down to kiss Kim on her lips and took a sip of her drink. "'Leena what up wit' you?"

"Hey Marcus." I leaned back into the cushion, and watched as Dollar walked right past me, like he didn't even see me. I grabbed my glass of Nuevo and downed it in one gulp.

"Girl what's wrong with you?"

"Dat mothafucka."

Standing up, I headed straight over to their section, where Dollar was seated. He, and his boys were rolling up blunts, popping bottles, and having a good time. I stood in front of the table, put my hand on my hip, and stared into Dollars eyes.

"You just gon' front on me like dat?! I'm invisible now?"

"Go back to your lil buddy." Dollar lit his blunt. "I'm tryna relax."

"Are you fuckin' serious right now?" Dollar took his bottle of Grey Goose to the head, then took a pull from his blunt, and blew a thick cloud of smoke in my face. Seeing a cup of something sitting on the table, I grabbed it, and threw it on him before he saw it coming. Everybody who were sitting at the table, jumped up to prevent from getting wet.

"Let me out."

I just stood there, and watched as Dollar came around the table. I thought he was going to blow on me, even hit me. But what he did, hurt me more than any blow could ever hurt. He walked right pass me and pulled that bitch Porsha into his arms. Talk about furious; I think my nostrils flared up; I was so heated.

The second Dollar let go, I punched her in her face, and seeing her stumble back, I took advantage. A punch to her eye, dropped her, and I was on her like a ufc fighter. Grabbing a hand full of her hair, I rammed her head into the floor continuously. I was crying and wasn't in control anymore. If it wasn't for Dollar pulling me off her, I probably would've killed her right then. That's just how mad I was.

"Girl chill yo' ass out!" Dollar yelled, as he tried to get me to stop swinging, and kicking the air.

"Let me go!"

"Cool out, and I will."

I stopped bucking for a minute, and when he let me go, I started throwing wild punches at him. He was bobbing, and weaving to keep his face from getting hit, but I was still throwing them. Out of nowhere, I was bare hugged from the back, and snatched off the floor. The whole time the bouncer carried me to the entrance I bucked, and talked shit; that is, until he put me outside. I just sat there on the ground and cried.

My girl Kim brought me my pouch, and helped me up, even wiped my eyes for me. She walked me to my Range, smoked a blunt with me, then told me she was riding with Marcus.

"You be careful, and let me know when ya get home ok?"

"I will…."

Sitting in the driver seat of my 2010 Range Rover Sport; I let out a muffled cry, as I wiped away my teary eyes. I was parked outside of my ex boyfriends condo, contemplating on rather or not I should go through with what I had planned. Visions of a drunken Dollar stumbling up the stairs to the front door of his condo, with his arms wrapped around my newest enemy, I quickly thought *fuck it*. I grabbed my best friend Kim butterfly knife from the glove compartment, then hopped out.

"I can do dis. I can do dis." I continued to tell myself, as I slowly walked up the driveway.

I made it to my destination moments later; Dollars 1976 Chevrolet Caprice Classic which was considered his prize possession. Flipping the knife open, I looked up at Dollars bedroom window, just as the lights were being shut off. With a slight smile, I keyed the words **FUCK YOU** on both sides of the car. I then stood back to admire my work. Impressed, but not satisfied, I slashed all four of the 28" tires sitting under the car. I felt better, my smile was wider, but knew I hadn't done enough yet; I wanted badly to hurt Dollar the way I'd been hurt.

Taking another glance up at Dollars bedroom window, I locked eyes with my enemy. With a quick roll of my eyes, I tried the driver side door handle. To my surprise, it was open. I began taking my anger out on the ostrich interior, slicing through the seats, the dashboard, even the convertible top. Happy, I slammed the door, and made a run for my SUV.

Before I could get out of the neighborhood good, my cellphone began to ring. The ringtone Papers by Usher, let it be known who was calling. Snatching my phone out of my Louis Vuitton bag, I answered, yelling; "what?!"

Dollar let out a laugh, one that irritated the shit out of me. Then said in his down south slang that truly comes out when he's mad; "I see yuh still on dat lil girl shit. Bitch grow da fuck up! Find yuh uh man and leave me da fuck alone. I'm through wit' chu. Yuh hea' me?! I'm done."

Dollar hung up, but I was determined I would get the last word. So, I called back, let it ring a few times then the voicemail picked up. I hung up.

"Ooooh, I hate chu!!!" I yelled out to no one, as I tried calling back.

Frustrated, and trying to figure out what I was going to tell Dollar, I paid no attention to the red light I was quickly approaching. By the time I did, it was too late. Passing through the four way, a Chevrolet Silverado 3500 rammed the driver side of my Range Rover. I watched in horror as my Range Rover spun around twice, then screamed while being rammed into a light pole. I was knocked unconscious due to the impact from the crash....

CHAPTER 16 DOLLAR

"Damn look what I don' did."

Looking down at 'Leena laid out in that hospital bed, with tubes of different medicines running into her body, I had to shed a tear. I was truly hurting inside, because I knew it was my fault, she was laying there in ICU. It was said she had a fifty-fifty chance of survival. Severe head trauma, a ruptured spleen, a couple of broken ribs on the left side, along with a broken left arm, and leg. Yeah, it was that serious. I continued to whisper encouraging words to try and uplift her spirits because I knew they were down.

Marcus, and Kim came to the hospital, Queen even flew in; Lord knows I was happy to see her. When Queen walked in, 'Leena was just waking up; one look at me, and she blew on me, but Queen calmed her down though. I tried talking to her, but the only words came from her mouth was leave. At first, I tried pleading with her, but when I noticed it was the waste of my time, I left. Kim, and Queen stayed to see about 'Leena; Marcus, and I sat in his Cadillac EXT smoking blunt after blunt, getting high.

We had a silent smoke session; there really wasn't anything to talk about. I wasn't really in the mood to do too much talking anyway, so we just kicked back, and vibed to the music playing through the factory speakers. My mind was on 'Leena. I wanted to apologize so bad, but I knew it wouldn't have changed anything. She was in the hospital because of my stupidity; some shit I could've prevented.

High as giraffe pussy, we ended up with the munchies, decided to go and get something to eat. I made a quick call to Queen, to see what they wanted to eat, but they didn't want anything. We headed to the well-known soul food restaurant in Knoxville, called Mama J's. Once we were seated, and our orders were placed, Marcus sparked up the conversation.

Leaning back in his chair, he looked over the table at me, and asked, "You aight? Or you still don't feel like talkin'?"

"I'm good my dude; I just been thinkin' dat's it."

"What's on ya mind?"

"Tryna figure out what imma do 'bout 'Leena crazy ass. I love dat mothafucka to death, but at da same time Porsha doin' somethin' to me. I ain't never knew dis shit was possible."

"What?"

The waitress came, and sat the plates down, along with the drinks, then left. As I munched down on my prime ribs, greens, macaroni & cheese, cornbread, with a sweet tea, I continued, "I ain't never knew you could be in love wit' two women at da same time."

"Oh shit. Man, you know I fuck wit' you da dumb way;" Marcus let out a little laugh. "But don't expect me to jump in it, when she tries to body yo ass. And you already know eventually it's what she gon' do. Either you, or Porsha."

"She crazy, but she ain't stupid."

"You remember dat Ms. Carolina shit, don't you? When old girl put uh hot one in her old man for tryna leave her for da side piece. He said da same shit…"

I didn't bother to respond, I just listened as I thought about what he said. When I didn't respond, Marcus shut up, and continued to eat. Once we were finished eating, we headed back to the hospital. On our way, I got a phone call from the babysitter telling me Jr. couldn't go to sleep and continued to yell about wanting his ma. I had Marcus take me to get him, and we went back to the hospital.

Not wanting Jr. to see 'Leena in the hospital, I let him sit in the car with Marcus while I went upstairs to say my goodbyes. When I stepped into the room, I gave my mama a hug and a kiss on the cheek, then I kissed 'Leena on the tip of her nose; she was asleep. Kim walked me back to where Marcus was parked, and we split up. I took Jr. to my spot, and put him to bed, then I laid in bed next to Porsha. After about an hour of lying there, staring at the ceiling, and talking to Porsha, I fell asleep.

□ They can't help it, and I can't blame 'em, since I got famous. They can't help it □

"Yeah." I reached over, and grabbed my cellphone off of the nightstand.

"Lil Brah. What up."

It only took me a second to realize who it was; Chuckaboy, my Big Brother. I knew he was supposed to be getting out soon on a life sentence parole, but I didn't know when. I climbed out of bed and headed to the bathroom. "Nigga what up. Way you at?"

"I jus' touch down in da Pote; way you at nigga?"

"I'm in Tenn uh key. But I'm 'bout to get ready to go to Miami. We have a game down dey. I want you to meet me down dey. I wonna see you."

"How? Nigga I ain't got no money."

"I know dat. But if you feel comfortable leavin' da state, all I need you to do is get to da airport."

"Comfortable? Fuck all dat. I heard 'bout you lil nigga. I want in, I'm tryna get paid. I'm 'bout to head to da airport now."

"Check. When you get dey, go to da desk, you will have a ticket waitin' on you. I'm 'bout to get my girl to order it now."

"Bet. Imma hit chu when I hit Miami."

"Fasho brotha."

After getting Porsha to handle that little business, I jumped in the shower. Once I finished washing, I got dressed, packed me a carry-on bag, then hit the streets. My first stop was to 'Leena's spot to see my mama, and Jr. then I headed to the hospital, to see 'Leena. It's been a few weeks since the accident, and she's been doing extremely well. But with the therapy, she wasn't expected to leave for another couple of months.

She continued to give me that nasty ass attitude. I took it, because I deserved it, but she was slowly breaking down. I stopped by to see her every day, picked up things from her school, that she needed to get her through the semester; the shit I was giving her, was the one thing I stopped giving a long time ago. Time. After making sure she was ok, I headed out to the college; we piled on the bus and headed out to the airport. A few hours later, we landed in Miami, Florida.

Walking through the lobby, I noticed Chuckaboy walking in my direction. Looking at him, was like looking in a mirror, we looked like identical twins, only he was a little taller, and bigger than I was.

"What up my nigga." Chuckaboy gave me a brotherly hug.

"I'm jus' coolin';" I stood back to look at him; he had to be 6'5" 280 solid. "Damn you done got big."

"I jus' been eatin' and workin' out. What da plans is?"

"Say bro." I heard Marcus call me.

I looked around, and when I spotted Marcus, I threw up the deuces, and headed in his direction. "What chu tryna do?"

"I'm tryna get some pussy and run dat sack up."

"Shit let's do it...."

☐ Hoes in the club showing love, shaking that ass in the club nigga wwhhhaaaattttt ☐

Sitting in Club Rolex, one of the topnotch strip clubs on the South Beach strip, I puffed on a blunt of some Jamaican Gold reefer and sipped on a bottle of Patron. Chuckaboy, Marcus, and Wayne were throwing money at the stage, while a thick ass pretty red bone freaked the pole. As usual, my mind was on some more shit; Big Bro stepped to me, told me to put him in the game, and I was trying to figure out which route I wanted to take.

I could've opened a reefer trap, let him start off with a few pounds, and slowly upgrade, but choosing the location was the thing. He couldn't go back to Savannah; he'd already violated his parole by skating out of town and wasn't worrying about going to see his PO. He was determined to run his sack up, and I was behind him with whatever he wanted to do. Deciding to play it how it come, I got my mind off that shit, and enjoyed my night.

A little stripper, who look like she wasn't no more than eighteen, came strutting past our table. A nice little 34c 26 38 frame, about 5'8", and a pretty smile with two cute golds in the front. Chocolate-complected, and I couldn't really see her eyes, but she had the kinky twist in her hair. She was looking good.

"Aye look here." I called out.

She looked at me and made her way to my side of the table; she sat down in my lap, "you must want a dance, callin' me like that."

Pulling out my knot of money, I pulled off a $100.00 bill, then gave it to her. "Nah, I really jus' wonna talk. You want somethin' to drink?"

Getting out of my lap, she sat down next to me. Looking at my bottle of Patron, she asked, "can I have some of that?"

I slid the bottle over to her, "you can have dat shit. Way you from?"

"Bartow."

"Bartow, Florida." I started busting a blunt to roll up. "I don' heard 'bout dat country ass shit. Uh bunch uh cows, and horses."

"Anyway nigga. My shit is not country." She laughed, knowing I was telling the truth. "Where you from?"

"I'm from Savannah lil mama."

"Oh ok. You're a Ga. Boy. What brought you to the bottom?"

"I play ball for Tennessee State. We have a game tomorrow. We playin' Miami. You should check it out. It starts at seven."

"I might just do that…"

"Marcus Pain has the ball. He's taking it down the court. Oh man; did you see that crossover?"

"I sure did Mike. I think he's going to take it in for the basket. He is, he's going up for the dunk."

"Kevin Dollar just pinned it to the backboard!!"

"That kid is freaking awesome. Reminds me of Jordan, with a little bit of Kareem Abdul-Jabbar."

Man, I was killing their ass, dropping them off left, and right with Tre's. And whenever I came into the paint, they got out of my way. Marcus couldn't even fuck with me; it didn't surprise me though, because after he took that bullet, he hasn't been the same. It was the second half, with eight minutes left to play, and we were up by eighteen; 68 to 50, I decided to take myself out of the game. It was Marcu's time to shine, and that's what he did. He broke that eighteen-point lead down to 6 in about six minutes.

With a couple of minutes left, I jumped back into the game. I wasn't trying to run that score back up; I was just trying to keep that lead; I did more passing than anything. When it was down to the last few seconds, I dribbled the ball slowly down the court, and threw it from half court; it went in. The crowd went crazy with cheers, as well as boos. We headed to the locker room to get changed, then we headed out the door.

Walking out the door, toward the parking lot, I noticed Marcus, Wayne, and Chuckaboy, leaning up against Marcus' EXT; he had it parked in front of the Hurricanes gym. We all dapped each other up and was about to hop into Marcus' SUV. A candy apple red painted drop top Chevrolet Caprice Classic pulled up. It caught our attention, but the driver caught mine. It was the lil stripper from the night before.

"Man, imma catch up wit' y'all niggas later."

"What?" That was Marcus.

"You puttin' me off bro. We need to talk." Said Chuckaboy.

"I'm already on top uh dat. Aye Wayne."

"Waah gwaan my bredren?" Asked Wayne.

"Dat lil thing we talked 'bout, give' it to bro. I got you. I'm gone."

CHAPTER 17 SALEENA

I finally made it out of the hospital and was doing good. Everything healed the way the doctors expected, but I still occasionally had pain all over. Dollar was back in the house, and he stayed every night; he also catered to my every need. If I mentioned anything about being hungry and he was home, he cooked. If he was running the streets, he stopped whatever he was doing, and bought me something to eat. Dollar massaged me all over every night, wanting to keep me from being in any pain.

Seeing him spend more and more time with Jr., so I could have some me time, had him gaining points with me. But I was still mad; more at myself, than I was at him. For falling in love with that nigga, giving him my all, believing in him, just to have my heart torn. *Where would things go from here?* I asked myself that all the time, but I wasn't about to give up on us. I was willing to try anything, to make things work with my man. The past was the past, and it didn't matter to me anymore.

As soon as I was released from the hospital, I was back working at the County Jail. I got on the first shift, the 6 a.m.-2 p.m., and I went to school at night. Monday, Wednesday, and Friday, I was in my criminology course, from 6 p.m-10 p.m., Tuesdays and Thursdays, I had the Criminal Law course. It seemed like Jr. had my schedule down to a T. Every morning, I awoke to the sound of his wining, him crying, and before I made it to his room, he met me in the hallway wiping his eyes.

My lil man was getting big. He was walking and trying to talk. We spoke two different languages, but I made him feel like I understood. For some reason, Jr. didn't like playing with too many toys, and we spoiled him with damn near every toy a baby boy would want to play with. He wanted to play with money. Jr. threw coins in the air, to see how high they would go, and threw cash in the air to watch it fly. Dollar continued to give it to him, and I sat back watching my baby grow into a Mini Dollar.

A few weeks after Jr.'s third birthday, I really paid attention to the transformation. He was the replica of Dollar. Everything Dollar did, he wanted to do. Everywhere Dollar went, Jr. tried to go. Dollar got him the little dreads put in his head, got him a baby chain, even a cute little baby ring, and kept him in the freshest baby gear.

After getting himself dressed in COOGI Sport, Dollar draped Jr. in Baby COOGI. I chose the pink pastel summer dress by Oscar De La Renta, with some fly sandals to match. Once we were all dressed, we headed to the other side of town; one of Dollars people were throwing a cookout and asked us to attend. I honestly didn't want to go, making new friends wasn't really my thing. But of course, you know if it meant spending time with Dollar, I was down for whatever.

The neighborhood where the party was had me mesmerized. There wasn't a home with anything less than five bedrooms. Everyone was stucco made, with huge windows in the front, manicured lawns, long driveways with some nice ass cars parked. I didn't ask any questions, I went with the flow, but in the back of my mind, I was wondering what the hell was going on. After riding down that long street, we finally made it to the dead end to where the party was.

We had to park on the street, because the driveway was packed. When we made it up the long driveway, and up the steps to the porch, Dollar rung the doorbell. A few minutes later, one of the double doors opened.

"Dollar." He opened the door, and dapped Dollar up. "It's good to see you my man. I'm glad you could make it."

"Dat what's up. Dis my lady Saleena, and dis my Jr." I shook his hand, and he smiled down at Jr. "Baby dis Romello. One uh my teammates who went pro."

"Oh ok. Congratulations."

"Thank You. Come on inside." We followed him inside. The foyer was huge, two sets of stairs lined the walls, and connected at the balcony. Like Tony's crib on Scarface. In the middle of the floor, was a fountain; it was a glass statute of Romello shooting a basketball. Water flew from the basketball, and into the fountain. Hanging from the ceiling, was a huge chandelier; everything was white, and gold. "There's plenty of food, drinks, games. I hope you enjoy yourselves."

Leading us through the house, Dollar and Romello talked. I began to wonder how it would feel to live in a home like that; eight bedrooms, five and a half baths, a theatre, a basketball court, the whole nine. Romello shit was laid out right. Stepping through the sliding back door, I knew it would be a long day; people were everywhere. I was ready to go just that fast.

Dollar gave me a deep kiss, and his usual warming smile, then started introducing me to everybody. Half of their names I forgot right after it was told to me; as I said, I wasn't into making too many new friends. Other than Kim, I didn't mess with too many females. Romello had a tent set up with several tables, and that's where we ate at. The whole time we ate, I was quiet; I wasn't feeling those sadity bitches. When Jr. mentioned the pool, I quickly got up, and walked him over to it.

He was about to jump into the water, like he saw a few of the big kids do, but I snatched him up before he could.

"He is so cute. How old is he?"

I looked around and spotted someone sitting on one of the steps in the 3 feet side of the pool; she had an adorable little girl standing in her lap, splashing water everywhere. I headed over to where she was, and after pulling Jr.'s clothes off, I sat down in the pool next to her.

"Jr. jus' turned three on da third." Jr., and her little girl was slashing water on each other, laughing uncontrollably. "I feel like he is goin' on thirty. He is growin' up so fast."

"Trust me, I know. This lil woman will be three in August, and think she run me."

"I thought I was da only one who had those problems. He so damn demandin'. I be forgettin' I'm da one in charge."

She let out a little laugh. "I feel you."

"Damn baby." We turned around and saw Romello standing there looking down at her. "You're going to sit out by the pool all day?"

"I don't like those bitches, and I'm not about to put up a front like I do. Those are your friends, not mine. So, to answer your question, yes, I am. Staying out here all day, until they leave."

"Dat goes for me too." I didn't associate myself with too many females, but for some reason she seemed cool to me. "Could you pass dat message to Dollah for me?"

"Sure, I can do that. But um," Romello pointed to the babies, "lil fresh being a lil to fresh with my Faith."

"Boy!" I turned around and caught Jr. leaning over; they looked like two grown-ups kissing. I guess he call himself doing what he sees his pops and I doing. I gave him the evil eye, and he smiled at me.

Looking over at Tracey I said, "I'm sorry 'bout dat."

"Sorry 'bout what?" Dollar walked up behind us; Jr. reached out for him, and of course Dollar grabbed him.

"Yo' son 'round here kissin' on lil girls."

"At least I know he ain't gay." Romello, and Tracey let out a little laugh.

"He only three years old Dollah." I was dead serious; I knew what was next to come.

Faith looked around, and seeing Jr. in Dollars arms, she had a fit; she started screaming, while reaching out for Romello. He got her from Tracey, and once Faith was in arms reach of Jr., she calmed down, and that smile of hers came back.

Dollar looked at me and smiled; "and he's a real ladies man."

I rolled my eyes, "Whateva…."

Dollar and Romello stripped down, then jumped in the pool with the babies; Tracey and I got out of the pool, and after drying off she showed me the house. After a bottom to top look through the house, we ended up in the kitchen at the island drinking. She poured us both a glass of Nuevo, and we chopped it up for a while. Of course, we talked about our niggas, but we were actually taking time getting to know one another. We may have had two different lives coming up, but we were damn near the same. When it was time to go, we exchanged numbers to keep in touch.

On the ride home from the party, Dollar argued with someone on the phone about some money; right then I knew I would be holding my pillow that night. When he pulled into the driveway to drop us off, I didn't bother saying anything. I just hopped out, grabbed Jr., and went into the house. Looking out the window, I saw him pull off. I just shook my head, then I got Jr. ready for bed. We played with his Lego's for a while, then I laid him down for the night.

Running myself some bath water, I decided to add a little bubbles, then I got into the tub. The water wasn't scorching hot, nor was it freezing cold; it was just right. I laid there in the tub for a while, just thinking; the water felt so good, it eased my mind, and I drifted off. A glass shattered somewhere in the house, and Jr. Screamed. Instantly I jumped out of the tub, grabbed my robe, and raced to see about my baby boy.

As I was running down the hall, I was tripped up by one of Jr.'s toys, he'd left by the guestroom door. By a handful of my hair, I was yanked up to my feet; that's when I noticed the other intruder standing there in front of me. He had Jr. in his arms with a gun to his head.

"Just give us what we want, and we'll leave." He stroked Jr.'s baby locks with the barrel of his 38 snub nose revolver.

"Aight." I looked from one to the other, "so what da hell y'all want?"

"The money out the safe."

Without a word I led them to the living room, and after taking down the family portrait posted on the wall of myself, Dollar, and Jr., I punched in the code to the safe. When it opened, I moved out of the way, and reached for my son. He gave Jr. to me, but kept a good eye on me, while his codefendant emptied the safe. They told me to lay face down on the floor, and a few minutes later they were gone. The first thing I did, was grab my phone to call Dollar, while I peeped out the window in search of a possible car they could be driving.

"What up mama." Dollar answered.

"Baby I need you." Laying Jr. down in my Queen size bed I decided to lay down with him. "Come home."

"I'm on my way...."

It took Dollar about fifteen minutes to get there; I was in the living room by then, just sitting on the couch, when he, and Chuckaboy stepped through the door. I jumped to my feet and wrapped my arms around his neck. That's when I broke down and started crying.

"Baby talk to me." Dollar took a step back, so he could take a good look at me; "what's wrong?"

"Somebody broke in da house."

"What?"

"Baby I'm sorry, dey got da money out da safe."

"Damn dat money." Dollar grabbed my chin, and turned my head from side to side; he was looking at my face, "did dey touch you?"

"Nah we good. But baby I ain't feelin' dis shit. Dey know way we stay."

"Cool out mama." Dollar grabbed me, pulled me into his arms, and hugged me tight, "I got you."

"Da house clean brotha." Chuckaboy had his 40. Cal out, with that killer look on his face.

"Aight." Dollar turned his attention back to me, "go pull ya car out, we goin' to my spot. Way my lil nigga at?"

"In da back."

"I got him. Meet me out front."

CHAPTER 18 DOLLAR

I had an addiction of getting money; slutting, stacking, and splurging. I couldn't help it; I was trapped in that d-boy life. I loved most of the things that came with it. The money got cars, clothes, women, houses, even brought arrogance to the table. With that, came hatred from envious niggas, and trifling bitches; that brought on beef. I ain't gon' flex, I ain't too tough like that beef shit; somebody always got killed, and I was scared that one of those bodies would be traced back to me.

Having one foot out, and one foot in the game, playing both sides of the fence; I was throwing rocks at the chain gang door, and didn't care. Damn being knee deep, I was neck deep in that water, I been had my feet wet. True enough, I didn't have to, but I liked selling work. The school thing was cool, but fucking with Wayne, and his nice ass numbers, I couldn't leave the dope alone. Buying ten keys for ten apiece, fronting them in the street for 20; I was seeing hella dough. The dope was good, 92% pure; I was taken those 10, turning them into 15; that's a 200 thou profit.

My dog Tron, ran through two, like it wasn't nothing; it took about a month, I shot him two more. Chuckaboy, I put him out in Memphis; opened a little trap house, and he started doing his thing, pushing three a month. It was time to re-up, I was out of work, and my niggas kept hitting me on my hip. I made a call to Wayne, and I was scheduled to get on a plane at 4:12 that evening. It was twelve in the afternoon.

I made a quick stop at Porsha spot, grabbed some money, and headed back to my condo. 'Leena was at work, so I knew I would be able to handle my business without hearing her mouth about me leaving the game. She tends to add on a lot of extra shit, I really don't be wanting to hear. Since the break in, 'Leena has been trying to get me to slowdown, but the money was coming too fast, I couldn't. Sitting back on the sofa, in the living room, I was running money through the money counting machine, to make sure I had Wayne's $100,000.00.

Chuckaboy had this little chick who drove the money down to Miami, and he was supposed to meet her in a few minutes to drop the money off on her. I finished counting the money, and had it packed in a duffel bag by 2:00 p.m... By the time 'Leena made it home, the money was gone, and I was kicked back, blowing on that gas, while watching Shottas.

"Hey baby." 'Leena bent down to give me a kiss, then sat down on the sofa next to me. "What chu been up to?"

"I jus' been coolin'. How was yo' day?"

"It was aight, borin' as usual. I can't wait to get on da force, hopefully it will be more exciting." 'Leena took her shoes off, threw her feet in my lap, and I gently began rubbing them.

"Let me ask you somethin'. Out of all da things you could be, why you want to be a police?"

"To keep you from gettin' in trouble. I'll be able to keep you on point wit' dem peoples."

"Oh really?"

"Yep." 'Leena straddled me and began kissing my lips; "I 'on't know what I'll do if dey take you away from us."

I lifted 'Leena's shirt over her head, and was about to unfasten her bra, but when my cellphone rung, she climbed down off me.

"Yeah, what up." I answered my cellphone, as I watched 'Leena walked toward our bedroom. I knew she was mad, hell I was back giving the streets more time than I was giving my family. I stayed on the go.

"Dis Kane cousin, you busy?"

"I'm jus' coolin'. What up family." I ain't talk to Kane in a minute. Last I heard, he was copping from Nico, and running the projects.

"I got cheddar, but I ain't got no pizzas to put it on."

"Way Nic' at?"

"He says he ain't fuckin' 'round nomo."

"Can you meet me in Miami tonight?"

"I'm 'bout to leave now. Imma hit you when I get dey."

"Bet."

After the phone call with Kane, I went and laid that pipe down to 'Leena. Once she was asleep, I took a hot shower, then I got dressed. I slid into a pair of dark blue jean shorts by LRG, a lite green LRG shirt, with LRG going across the front in white, with some white, and lime green Air Max 95's. Putting my gold Marc Jacobs wristwatch on my wrist, my phones in their holster on my hip, I was ready to go.

I kissed 'Leena on the tip of her nose, then I jetted out the door. On the way to the airport, I called Chuckaboy to let him know I was about to take off. I also called Porsha. Since the night of 'Leena's accident, we haven't been seeing too much of one another, but we have been keeping in touch. After promises of us getting together when I got back, I ended the call, and went to catch my flight.

A few hours later, I landed in Miami. Marcus was at the airport waiting for me, when I arrived. As I made my way to the 1971 Chevrolet Corvette Marcus was parked in, I made the call to Wayne to let him know I made it in town; he told me to meet him at his restaurant.

"What up bro." I hopped into the passenger seat, and dapped Marcus up.

"I'm coolin' my dude. What da business is?" Marcus asked, as he pulled out.

"Take me to bro spot."

"Fasho."

Island Breeze bar & grill; an upscale Jamaican restaurant, Wayne opened at the beginning of the year, stayed packed; mostly with dreads. It was out there on South Beach, right on the strip, between the Hilton, and the Marriott hotels. The décor was black, green, and yellow, representing Jamaica to the fullest. Walking through the double glass doors, we stepped into a spacious room, the size of an I Hop. Tables were scattered out everywhere, with two or more chairs around them. In the middle of the floor, was a circular bar, with several barstools around it.

Wayne was seated at one of the tables on the far-right side in the back, by the stairs; they were leading up to his office. When we approached the table, he stood and smiled.

"Waah gwaan bredren." Wayne shook my hand and pulled me in for a brotherly hug.

"I'm just coolin' round."

"Wah bout yuh?" Wayne asked, giving Marcus a brotherly hug.

"I can't holla." Marcus proudly stated.

"Cum inna." Wayne led us upstairs to his office; we took a seat on the couch. "Wah yuh wa fi jink?"

The office was laid out, more like a lounge spot, than an office. There was a couch that circled the wall to the left. On the wall across from that, was a huge tv. On the back wall was a mini bar he kept stocked, and in the middle of the floor, was a long glass table.

"Remi and Sprite." Pulling a blunt out of my pocket, I busted it, and rolled up some Jamaican Gold reefer.

"Henn and coke." Marcus grabbed the remote off the couch and turned the tv on.

Wayne grabbed his walkie talkie from his hip, said some shit quick, and within a few minutes, a fine ass amazon came in. She mixed our drinks, and after sitting them on the table, she left. Grabbing our drinks, we all sat back down on the couch. I lit up my blunt, Wayne turned the tv up, and looked over at me.

"Now wah yuh wa fi chat bout?"

"I got a hundred on da way for dem ten." I hit the blunt real hard and passed it over to Wayne. "But I need you to throw me ten mo' and separate da two packs. One uh my folk on da way from da pote to get dem from me. Imma send you dat money when I get back."

"Suh yuh wa twenty???" Wayne nodded his head up and down, while slowly rubbing his hands together. "Dis a wah mi a duh fi yuh. Mi a gi yuh twenty-five fi two. Yuh tink yuh cya handle it?"

"Nigga if you put fifty in my hand, imma handle it."

Wayne laughed and shook my hand. "Mi like di way yuh tink. Gimme a call lata, an mi wi get yuh right. Yuh check?"

"Check."

When Kane made it in town, we met up at the Club Rolex, to chop it up. I told him about the ten keys, and he told me about the fifty g's he brought with him. I got his money, dropped him the ten keys, and charged him fifteen apiece; told him to get at me when he got them off, because I needed that other one hundred. I spent the rest of my night with the cute little stripper chick Melanie, I met the last time I was in the bottom. I woke up early the next morning; Chuckaboy little chick called to let me know she made it, and after getting the money, I packed her down, gave Wayne his money, then hopped on a flight back to Tennessee.

I made it home around five that evening. 'Leena was laid out in bed, with Jr. little ass next to her; they were watching something on tv. The minute I stepped through the bedroom door, Jr. jumped up, ran across the bed, and dove into my arms. 'Leena started smiling, and I made my way around to her side of the bed. "How you doin'?" I leaned in and kissed her lips.

"Betta now." 'Leena gave me that, why you keep leaving me alone, look. I sat down on the edge of the bed next to her. Before I could open my mouth, she continued. "I 'on't wonna hear it baby, you here now. You ate yet?"

"Nah. Y'all ate?"

"Earlier."

"Get dressed, I'm in da mood for some chicken fingers, and ribs." I looked down at Jr. who was standing in my lap, trying to pull my chain over my head, "how dat sound?" He shrugged his shoulders, "nigga what up? You aight? You 'on't wonna kick it wit cha daddy?"

"Dada have some money?" He had my chain over my head and around his neck. He had his hand out smiling.

"Imma let chu handle dat, I'm 'bout to get ready." 'Leena got out of bed and went to get an outfit from the walk-in closet.

Pulling my money out of my pocket, I sat Jr. down on the bed next to me. "How much money you want?" He snatched my knot, threw it, then laughed. "Oh, dat's how ya feel?" I bent down to pick the money up.

"Nigga don't blame him. Its yo' fault he makin' it rain."

"You just get dressed, don't worry 'bout what's goin' on ova here. I got dis."

"Whateva."

After waiting about an hour for 'Leena to get dressed, we finally made it out the door. Applebee's has the best chicken finger, and rib combo, so that's where we ended up at. We got a booth, on the left side of the restaurant, and after being seated, we placed our orders. When the meals first made it to the table, 'Leena was eating like she was hungry, but out of the blue she looked as if she'd lost her appetite. I guess she didn't expect me to peep the move; I leaned back into the cushion.

"You aight ma?" I had one eyebrow raised.

"I think I know who broke into da house."

"What?! Who?!" I was turning to look around the restaurant.

"Baby don't look. I'm lookin' right at him, he a few booths down wit' some chick. Dey had on mask, but baby I will never forget dat tattoo he had on his neck."

"You sure?"

"One hundred percent, and if I ain't know no betta, I will say dat's Kim he wit."

"I got use bathroom;" said Jr.

"Take him to da bathroom and let me know what da deal is."

"Aight. Come on lil man."

I pulled my phone out of its holster on my hip and called Chuckaboy. After telling him what was going on, he told me he would be up there in a few minutes, then ended the call. Not once did I look back to see who 'Leena was talking about; I waited for her to return, to confirm what she suspected. When she did, I gave her my car keys, and told her to take off. A few minutes later Chuckaboy called, and told me he was outside; I headed out to the parking lot, and to the car he was parked in.

"What up bro?" I pulled a blunt out of the box of blunts sitting on the dashboard and busted it down to roll up some reefer.

"Way dat fuck nigga at?" Chuckaboy checked the clip, then pushed it back in, and cocked his 40 caliber.

"He still inside, but listen;" I lit the blunt up, "we ain't 'bout to fuck wit' him right now. I want dat bitch he wit'. I know her, and I'm 'bout to use dat to my advantage. Dey dey go. Follow 'em at a distance, let's see way dey go at."

They hopped into a Chevrolet Suburban, and when they pulled out of the parking lot, Chuckaboy pulled out after them. I thought they were going to go across town or something, but they didn't; they pulled into a hotel, only a few blocks from Applebee's. Chuckaboy slowly turned into the parking lot, and I spotted the Suburban backing into a parking space in front of one of the room doors. Chuckaboy rode past and found a parking space. I was able to see the Suburban from where we were parked, along with their room door.

They were in the room for a couple of hours; we sat in the 2006 Monte Carlo and got high, while we waited on the door to open. When it finally did open, I watched as only one of them came out, and it was the nigga who hopped into the Suburban. I waited for him to pull out, then I hopped out, and went to knock on the door.

"Damn dat was fast." She opened the door without even asking who it was. When she saw me, she put her hand on her hip. "What chu want Dollah?"

"For you to get dressed and bring yo ass on."

"Way, we goin'?" She began getting dressed.

"Not to Marcus. I got a job for you."

I had Kim to call that nigga and set up a flaw lick. The spot we chose was an abandoned house, not too far away from the trap house, where Chuckaboy trapped out of. I paid a couple of young niggas from the neighborhood, who've been trying to get down with us since we opened the spot. They were to handle the business. Leaving Chuckaboy to oversee the whole mission, I took off with

Kim.

We ended up at a hotel waiting for 'Leena to arrive. I wanted to see her beat Kim's ass, for more reasons than one. Sitting back in one of those chairs at the table by the window, I smoked on a blunt of dro; Kim paced back and forth. When I heard the knock on the door, I looked over at Kim, and she opened the door. 'Leena stepped in, completely ignored Kim, and sat down in a chair next to me.

"What up." She took the blunt from me and took a puff.

"I'm waitin' now." I pulled my phone out of its holster and sat it down on the table. "It shouldn't be too much longa."

"I knew it was somethin' 'bout dem niggas when I saw 'em in dat club. I felt uh vibe."

"Who you talkin' 'bout?"

"Dem niggas who tried to talk to us at yo party." 'Leena jumped to her feet, like she about to charge Kim. I grabbed her hand. "And dis bitch was bein' real friendly. Wit da nigga who put a gun to my son's head!!"

"I know you 'on't think I had somethin' to do wit' dat shit!" 'Leena folded her arms across her chest, and cut her eyes at Kim, "oh for real. Bitch we go way back. I will neva do no shit like dat to you."

Right then my cellphone began to ring; I snatched it up. "What's good brotha?"

"Dat shit dey done. He says some bitch name Kim set it up."

"Fasho my nigga. Dat's what I was waitin' on. Imma fuck wit' you lata."

"Yeah."

I ended the call, looked over at 'Leena, and nodded my head up, and down. 'Leena jumped to her feet, and this time I didn't stop her. Kim jumped off the bed and squared up.

"Hol' up 'Leena, it ain't what you thinkin."

"Bitch!" 'Leena threw a right hook; Kim bobbed, ducked it, and caught 'Leena with a left jab to her mouth. It started bleeding, but 'Leena kept going; she caught Kim with a three-piece combo; right, left, right jabs. "You thought you did somethin'?"

'Leena caught Kim with a knee to her stomach, and Kim dropped to her knees, holding her stomach. 'Leena was about to punch her again, but Kim held one of her hands out. "Leena I ain't know you was home." 'Leena punched Kim in her face again. She took it and continued to stare at 'Leena. "I just wanted to get dat nigga back."

"What?" 'Leena stepped back but kept her eyes on Kim.

"I was pregnant 'Leena." Kim arose to her feet; "me, and Dollah."

Before she could finish her statement, 'Leena was on her. 'Leena gripped Kim's neck with her left hand and hit Kim with a right elbow to her face; twice. She dropped down to her knees again. This time 'Leena didn't stop. She punched Kim in the face until I pulled her off Kim.

"Dollah let me go." The shit I heard in her voice, I knew she was serious; I let her go, waited for her to blow on me. She punched me in my mouth, then pointed her finger in her face; "you wonna fuck my best friend? Go 'head. I hope she got a place for you to stay. Don't come home, and nigga I mean dat shit."

I ain't say nothing; I just watched as 'Leena walked over to where Kim was stumbling to get up. 'Leena punched her in her face, dropping her back down to the ground, then she walked out.

CHAPTER 19 SALEENA

Dollar fucked Kim; I never saw that one coming. It hurt me to my heart, the way I was betrayed. My best friend, my first, and my only love; I didn't know what to do, where to go, nor who to trust. What I did know was, I needed a drink. Ending up on the East side of Memphis, I was at Wet Willie's, taking shot after shot of Tequila, trying to drink away my pain. For every set of tears I shed, I downed a shot; by my fourth one, I was drunk, but I kept going.

Several niggas tried to get at me, but the chump off got worse, and louder every time. Eventually they left me alone, to soak in my own misery. When the bartender realized I could no longer control myself, he quit giving me shots, told me I was drunk, and that it was time to go. Knowing I wasn't able to drive, I pulled my cellphone out of my pocket, to call Tracey, and see if she would come and get me. We've been staying in touch since we met, even went out a few times, and we've become rather tight.

The screen on my phone was blurry, I couldn't see anything, but I managed to make it to my phone contacts. I strolled through it, made it to the end, started over, and pushed send. I was hoping it was Tracey's number I was calling.

"Hello." My eyes went wide, it wasn't Tracey. That voice was too deep, and sexy. I didn't say anything, the phone was glued to my ear. "Baby girl what up, way ya at?"

"At Wet Willie's, can you come and get me?" My words were slurred; I knew he knew I was drunk. I was hoping he had better things to do, because I was having some crazy thoughts. Payback is a bitch, and that's exactly what I was thinking about getting.

"Gimme uh few, imma be through dey."

"Aight." I hung up with the quickness. The liquor had me about to say some things I knew I would regret later.

I sat there at the bar waiting; a thousand different thoughts ran through my mind. The scene at the hotel with Dollar, and Kim, continued to pop up. That sexy ass voice on the phone, along with the body to match, threw a devious smile on my face. When I heard some loud music coming up the block, I knew it was him; grabbing my things, I headed out the door. When the candy apple green 1962 Buick Electra 225 convertible, sitting up on them chrome 24" rims, pulled up in front of the door, I hopped in.

"Roll up," Was the only thing he said. Tossing me a blunt, and an ounce of reefer, he pulled out.

I leaned back in the seat, and up against the door. Rolling up a blunt of purple haze, I caught a glimpse of him out of the corner of my eye. That nigga was black as night, some call it blue black. If it wasn't for the street's lights, and his iced-out grill, I could fool myself to think the car was driving itself. I reached into my pocket to grab my lighter, but he passed me his. I lit up the blunt, hit it a couple of times, then passed it.

"So, you gon' tell me what's goin' on?" His lungs were full of smoke, but he still hit it a couple more times, then passed it back to me. I really didn't know how to respond; my hormones were starting to take over. I just sat back, hit the blunt, and kept quiet. He continued, "I guess not. Shit, it's cool."

With the remote he held in his hand, he flipped through the songs on the mp3 player built in his CD player, and once he found what he was looking for, he turned the volume up. He kept it at a decent volume, so if I wanted to talk, he could hear me. All I wanted to do is cry, and that's what I did. Choices, by Monica, and Keyshia Cole, played through the speakers, and all I thought about was Dollar's trifling ass. Looking over at me, he saw me wiping my eyes, and shook his head.

"Talk to me 'Leena." He passed me another blunt. I already had the reefer, so I began to roll it up. "Why yo' pretty ass ova dey droppin' dem tears, gettin' drunk and shit?"

"I'm hurting." The tears began to rain uncontrollably. "I'm sick of dat nigga fuckin' me ova. I'm so confused right now."

I paused to finish rolling the blunt, and I heard him say, "I'm listenin'."

I lit the blunt and was so caught up by the attention I was getting, I wasn't thinking about the fact we were getting on a highway. I just kept on talking. "I love him, but I hate him. Want to leave him, but I can't live wit' out him. You know what I'm sayin'?"

"Yea I feel you. But check dis, I ain't no hatin' ass nigga. Its uh million things I could tell you right now, but dat ain't my thing. Da only thing imma say is, go wit' your heart. It may lead you in da wrong direction; I know, I been dey, but it could lead you way you tryna go." He reached over and lifted my chin up. "You gon' be aight lil one. Keep ya head up."

The shit he was saying sounded good, but that liquor, that reefer, his smile, along with his touch; he had my juice box wet. I wanted to climb on top of him right then and there. I decided to pick his brain a little bit.

"Can I ask you a question?"

"If it's on yo mind, don't hol' it in."

"Do yo' fine ass have an old lady?"

"Old lady, nah. But I do have women I occasionally fuck. Since I been out, I really ain't been looking for one. My focus is runnin' dat check up, makin' show I'm straight, den I will get to dat point."

"Oh ok. So, are you into one-night stands?"

"You 'on't tell, I won't." He turned into the driveway of a nice two-story brick home. We were somewhere in Nashville.

I sat there for a moment, trying to figure out what to say to that. I threw the bait out, he bit, and I couldn't cop out. Well, I could've, but I didn't want to. When he hopped out, and said "come on in", I got out, and followed him inside. The décor of the interior was relaxing; white walls, thick tan carpets, tan living room sets to match; I asked, "is dis yo' spot?"

"Yep." He grabbed the remote off of the living room table and turned the 53" plasma tv on. "Make yourself at home. You want somethin' to drink? Cool aid, sweet tea, water, Moet, Patron, Goose?"

The shit that I had planned, I knew I would need some liquor. "Let me get uh cup of Goose; straight."

He grabbed a box of Swisher sweets off the top of the tall speaker on the side of the entertainment system and tossed it to me. I sat down on the couch, as he said, "roll a couple up. I'm 'bout to grab dat drink for you."

By the time I finished rolling up a couple of blunts, he was walking back into the room. He sat the drinks down and sat next to me on the couch. I passed him one of the blunts, and while he lit it up, I grabbed the remote off the table; I didn't want to watch tv, I wanted to listen to music. I turned the tv off and turned the stereo on. I like, by Jeremiah, started playing. I took a gulp of my drink and sat down in his lap."

At first, I was just grinding on him, dancing to the beat, but then his dick started to harden under me. I got into it, trying to make myself climax. When I accomplished my goal, I turned around, and straddled his lap; he tried to pass me the blunt, I declined, and continued my dance. I lifted his Polo shirt over his head, then his wife beater. I ran my hands up, and down his chiseled chest, then wrapped my arms around his neck; I kissed his lips.

The first couple of kisses were just pecks, then our tongues had a fight. We were heating up, then a glimpse of Dollar popped into my mind. I pulled away and stared at him; I knew I wasn't supposed to be there. He rubbed my back, my neck, and ran a hand through my hair. I got off of him and sat on the couch.

"You aight?" He took a sip of his Moet.

"Yea I'm good." I grabbed my cup, took another gulp, then stood up. Reaching out for his hand, he allowed me to pull him to his feet. "Let's go upstairs."

I led the way up the stairs, and past the first two rooms; I made my way to the master bedroom, as if I knew exactly where I was going. Entering the room, I pushed him down on the bed, and climbed on top of him. I kissed his lips, sucked on his neck, then nibbled on his ear. I knew it was turning him on, his hands finally started moving. He lifted my shirt over my head, then unfastened my bra; my breast popped out at him. He grabbed them both, and slowly caressed them, slowly squeezing them.

He took them in his mouth one by one, while I danced on his dick, through his shorts. Grabbing his hands, I put them together, and held them over his head, with one hand. I kissed and licked my way down his chest. Licking his belly button, I blew in it, to dry it up, and kept moving down. As I was reaching my hand in his shorts to pull his dick out, visions of me sucking Dollar's dick came to mind; I pulled my hand out of his shorts and sat down on the edge of the bed.

He scooted behind me, with his legs spread on either side of me, and I felt his dick slide against my ass. His warm breath on my neck, the softness of his lips nibbling on my ear, sparked up something inside of me. Dollar disappeared from my mind at that moment. Leaning back into his arms, he held me tight for a moment, before laying me down on my back. Sliding my shorts down, then my panties, he showered my body with kisses from my ear to my feet, then back up to my breast.

Licking around my nipples, he made his way to the underside of my breast, while the whole time playing with my clit. It was feeling so good, I started grinding my hips against his hand, and he stuck two

165

fingers in my pussy. He continued to finger fuck me, licking his way down my body, to my clit. He flicked my clit with his tongue, and I moaned, damn near climaxed just off that.

"Oh shit!" I yelled with excitement.

That nigga knew what he was doing. Finger fucking me slow, hooking my g spot, and sucking on my clit. Gripping the back of his head, I pushed his face deeper into my pussy. I was climaxing, and he was sucking it all up.

"Don't stop. Oh shit. Nigga I'm cummin'. Right dey!" I was grinding my pussy against his face, trying to keep up with his rhythm. "Right dey! Oh, shiiiiit I'm cummin'. I'm cummin."

He came up for air, and I was trying to catch my breath. He kissed my lips, and I didn't mind tasting my own juices; I licked it from his lips. He pulled a condom out of his shorts pocket, took his shorts off, then pulled off his boxers. When I saw those 12", I was like oh shit. Watching him slide the condom on, I was trying to build up my confidence. That's when he placed the head at the entrance of my heavenly gates.

"Hol' up." I put my hands out and touched his chest. Realizing that wasn't the best move, I dropped my hands to my side. Dollar popped back into my mind, bringing up memories of the first time we had sex. I was about to cop out, but visions of Dollar fucking Kim popped into my mind. I reached out, stroked the length of his dick, then smiled up at him. "Come on. I'm ready."

"You show?"

"Yeah...."

I awoke the next morning, to the bright sun shining in through the tall window in the bedroom. The headache I had was worse than any of the others I've had in the past. It seemed as if the pounding would start at both temples and meet at the middle of my brain. The light beaming into my eyes wasn't helping at all. I got out of bed to close the blinds, and that's when the reality of me being naked hit. Quickly searching the room, I found my clothes in a pile, and sat on the edge of the bed to put them on.

Scenes from the night before began to replay in my mind. I tried to remember everything that happened but couldn't. Only bits, and pieces. *Did I fuck him?* I continued to ask myself, because that's one of the parts I didn't remember. My pussy wasn't sore, but it was damn sure sticky, and by the size of that nigga I knew if I did, I would still have been feeling it.

Trying to think on it too hard, my brain started beating harder. I covered my eyes, and my forehead with both of my hands, hoping to relieve the tension. That didn't work, so I said fuck it. Needing to use the bathroom, I got up, and headed for the door. As I was making my way to the bathroom, I heard voices coming from downstairs. I eased my way over to the staircase, to do a little eavesdropping.

Damn, dat's Dollar, I thought listening to Dollar complain to Chuckaboy. 'She ain't come home last night, she ain't answering her phone, man I don't know way she at'. That's what I heard Dollar saying, and after looking around, seeing that I was in Chuckaboy's house, was in his bed last night, letting him taste my goods, I felt bad. Not bad enough to run down the stairs and tell on myself. I knew Dollar to well, and with the temper he had, he would probably try and kill me.

I was happy when Chuckaboy let Dollar out; I damn near ran to the bathroom, trying not to pee on myself. Happy I made it in time, I took care of my business, and once I was finished, I searched the medicine cabinet for a new toothbrush. After finding a pack, I brushed my teeth, ran me a bath, grabbed a towel, and a rag from the bathroom closet, then sat in the tub.

The knocking on the door, knocked me out of my trance. I jumped, then settled back down just as quickly. I continued to bathe; "what up?"

"Bro gon'," Chuckaboy walked in, and took a seat on the toilet; he looked me straight in the eye. "What chu tryna do? Way you tryna go?"

"Did we have sex last night?" I wanted to know.

He gave me the same half smile as Dollar, and I had to look away. "As bad as I wanted to tear yo' lil fine ass up, I didn't. You went out on me. Now answer my question."

"I need to get somethin' to eat, den you can take me to my car."

"Dat what's up. I will have you somethin' ready by da time you get out."

"Ok."

Once I devoured the beef sausage, grits, eggs and biscuits Chuckaboy put together, he dropped me off at my car. I really didn't have a destination, I just rode around, and got high as I thought about all the current chain of events. My mind was so cluttered, trying to predict what was next to come my way, was impossible. After finishing my second blunt, I decided to head out to the condo; Jr. was at the babysitters, so I knew he was in good hands, and not in the mood to deal with him, I decided to leave him there until I made it home and got myself together.

As I was pulling up to the condo, my cellphone began to ring, then it beeped letting me know it was going dead. Throwing the car in park, I answered it, while placing it on the car charger. "What up homie." It was Tracey.

"Girl where are you!?!" There was this urgency I heard in her voice.

"That boy Dollar just left here. Dropped lil man off and said some shit about trying to find you. What the hell is going on? Where are you?"

"At home, well sittin' outside in da car."

"In the car? Why are you in the car?"

"I was jus' pullin' in when ya called, but check dis, I'm 'bout to run upstairs, and try to get myself together. Den imma swing through dey."

"That's cool. I'll see you when you get here."

"Aight."

"Bye."

I hung up, grabbed my phone, pocketbook and headed upstairs. It was quiet inside and dark; all the shades were closed, so I knew Dollar wasn't home. I made my way to our bedroom and sat down at the edge of the bed. Taking off my shoes, then my clothes, I went to take me a shower. I felt so dirty, I scrubbed my body, then let the water sprinkle down on my body for a few minutes.

Stepping out of the shower, I saw Dollar leaning up against the bathroom counter, going through my phone. I snatched a towel from the rack and began to dry off. I then remembered that I didn't erase Chuckaboy's number from my call log. When I turned around, shit popped off.

"Bitch chu fuckin' my brotha?" He slapped me across my face so hard, I fell to the floor. I tried to get up, and plead my case, but he slapped me again, and read a text message from my phone aloud, "we should get together again some time. Let me know when you free."

"Dollah it ain't what"

He punched me in my face, and when it landed, I saw nothing but blackness for a minute. When I opened my eyes, I realized Dollar was pulling me up by my hair. That nigga threw me into the full-length mirror on the wall, and the second I was up on my wobbly legs, I fell back down to the floor. I wanted to fight back, but I couldn't; I didn't have any energy. I just cried as he stood over me, beat the shit out of me, and call me all types of names.

He slapped the shit out of me one more time, then spit on me. "Dat's why I'm 'bout to get married you stupid bitch."

All the energy I figured he beat out of me, came back when he said that, and I slowly made it to my feet. By the time I made it to the bedroom, I saw Dollar headed to the front door. I quickly grabbed, then covered myself in a robe. Grabbing my car keys, one of Dollars

40 Cal's he kept in a shoebox, on the shelf in the top of the closet, I headed out the door. He was already in his car pulling out when I made it outside; I hopped in my Benz and followed him.

Either he knew I was following him, and just didn't care, or he really wasn't paying attention. When he pulled into the neighborhood called Hillcrest, he bent a few blocks then pulled into the driveway of a nice stucco made home. One of several dozen homes in the upscale neighborhood.

"Take yo' ass on someway 'Leena." Dollar yelled stepping out of his car. He was staring straight at me, with a mug on his face that I've never seen before.

I was only going to hop out and flash the gun, but when I saw that bitch Porsha step out the front door yelling, "why you brought that bitch to my house?" Something totally different crossed my mind. I cocked that 40. Cal, and hopped out shooting. I pulled the trigger twice, letting two bullets fly in Porsha's direction. Dollar took off running across the lawn, and I started letting loose.

"I hate chu!" I was chasing Dollar, letting bullets fly after him. *If I can't have you, nobody will,* I thought. I continued shooting, paying no attention to the little boy trying to make it to the front door of his home, only a few houses down. Letting off the eighteenth shot, emptying the clip, I was only a few feet away from the little boy lying on the ground. My eyes locked on him, then at the gun I was holding in my hand. A young black teenage girl came running through the front door screaming.

"Somebody help! My brothers been shot!" Dropping to her knees, she slid the little boys head in her lap.

For a second, I just stood there staring at the scene. Someone yelled, "lookout she's got a gun!" That's when the approaching sirens rung in my ear. Knowing I was going to jail if I was caught, I took off running to my car. Hopping in, I started the ignition, and pulled off.

The neighborhoods entrance was blocked off by a couple of police cruisers, with a couple of officers standing in front of them; they had their guns pointed in my direction. I had run out of options, and wasn't about to try that Set it Off, ramming through cars shit. I killed the engine and placed my hands on the steering wheel as instructed. Within seconds I was snatched out of the car, handcuffed, and placed into the backseat of one of the police cruisers. Once I was transported to the Blount County Jail, I was charged with first degree murder.

I sat in the county jail for a little over six months. In that time, I went to my bond hearing, and the $100,000.00 bond, my $20,000.00 lawyer tried to get me, was denied. During the preliminary hearing, the murder charge was thrown out, due to a technicality found by my lawyer; it wasn't the bullet from my gun that killed the little boy. During surgery, the surgeon mistakenly hit a major artery, and that was the cause of death. Having the murder beat, I thought I was about to go home, but boy was I wrong.

I was hit with a hot track, one count of aggravated assault with a deadly weapon. That bitch Porsha pressed charges, then hit the stand crying and shit. Telling how I shot at her. Dollar's name never came up, and through the entire process he was nowhere to be found. After a long heavy discussion with my lawyer, I ended up copping out to a 10 do 5 years plea deal, for the aggravated assault, and possession of a firearm. I sat in the county for a few months, then was sent off to prison to serve my time.

ABOUT THE AUTHOR

Brandon Young is a native of Savannah Ga. Born to Joseph Young JR. and Linda Young, on January 16, 1986. He was the youngest of three, and the toughest to deal with. With a passion for writing, he began with short poems, and music lyrics at an early age. Yes, he was Blessed with many talents, from football, basketball, to baseball. But by his teenage years none of those kept his attention; he found his way to the streets. Which cost him all of his twenties, and the beginning of his thirties to the state of Ga. Department of corrections. After a lengthy sentence, Brandon Young has found his way back to his passion for writing, and with one novel published, another on the way he is what one would consider a Convict turned Author.